BOOBS

A Tale of American Politics and a Girl

SIMON PLASTER

Copyright 2015 by Simon Plaster

All rights reserved. Published by Mossik Press.

mossikpress@mail.com

Library of Congress Cataloguing-in-Publication Data

Plaster, Simon [12.9.2015]

Boobs: A Tale of American Politics and a Girl
by Simon Plaster

p. cm

ISBN 978-0-991-44805-0

1 . Humor—Fiction.
2. Oklahoma, United States—Fiction.
3. Politics—Fiction.
4. Gender—Fiction.
I. Title

10 9 8 7 6 5 4 3 2 1

Manufactured in the United States of AmericaFirst Edition

BOOBS

A Tale of American Politics and a Girl

SIMON PLASTER

MOSSIK PRESS

I

WHAT'S IN A NAME?
William Shakespeare/Romeo & Juliet

⊙NE

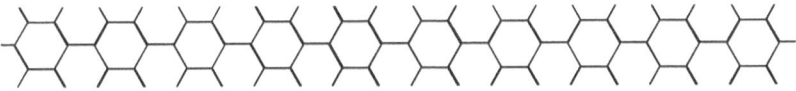

Henryetta sat at her desk in the storefront office of the *Weekly Herald*—a small town newspaper—mindlessly opening mail. There was no news to report, not like in the last election season, when a lot was going on in her little ol' Oklahoma hometown, also named Henryetta. Back then, she her own self was first to report that Virgil Carter, an unfamous pots-and-pans salesman from a nearby town, was running for County Commissioner, as a Democrat! That was unusual as rain in August for Okmulgee County, and caught the attention of politicians and newspapers all the way to Washington, D.C. Overnight, Virgil became what they called a "darling" to them, and to her mother, Wynona Sue, too. He was a smooth out loud talker alright, and Oklahoma was what they described as "in play" for the Presidential election, which must have been the reason Virgil got picked to be on the ballot for Vice-President of the United States. He promised he would take her mother up to Washington with him, but…

At the recollection of Wynona Sue getting her heart broke by Virgil Carter, Henryetta's mind drifted farther back in time to when Gaylord Goodhart, the love of her own life, gave her the mitten—her mother's old-fashioned term for being rejected by the one you wanted. Gaylord, a star football player, and she, a cheerleader, had been one of the cute couples in high school, and might have got married after graduation, but… Henryetta sighed. Gaylie turned semi-rotten during their Senior year and went to prison down in Texas 'stead of college at Murray State University over in Tishomingo. She never believed a word about what they said he did to that gal in Oklahoma. And her reporting about how he later got framed again, so he would have to play bigtime football for the Texas State Penitentiary Chain Gang, no doubt had somethin' to do with him getting out of jail, but...

A tear ran down Henryetta's slightly freckled cheek, as she vividly recalled falling to the ground in front of the court house steps. Through watery eyes she again saw Gaylord standing above her with open arms. Before he could bend down and lift her up, his teammate, Billy Ray Williams—also sprung from prison—ran into Gaylie's embrace. She saw them hug, then kiss, on the lips, with open mouths. Yep, Gaylord Goodhart definitely gave her the mitten, then went on to become the greatest college football player in history. Now he was a star studback for the Dallas Cowboys.

Hardly able to believe that Gaylie —still the love of her life—was really gay, Henryetta again sighed, put aside morbid thoughts about what might have been, and went back to the dull routine of opening mail and waiting for something to happen.

Her mother, Wynona Sue, never would have got to Washington, D.C. with Virgil Carter even if he had not took up with another gal, as things turned out. Democrats and Republicans were deadlocked about almost everything last time around, especially about whether the President ought to be elected by popular vote or by Electoral College votes like the Constitution said. Both parties changed positions back and forth, depending on what the polls predicted from time to time. But some states, led by California's example, had got locked in by their laws—made up to get around the Constitution—that obliged them to cast their Electoral College votes for whichever candidate got the most popular votes nationwide. The result was what they called a real snafu. 'Cause when the popular vote came in at almost a tie — within margins that in a lot of states would have made recounts automatic — they had to add up again the whole nationwide total of almost two-hundred million popular votes. And had to keep on re-recounting them when the bottom lines came out different every dern time.

Henryetta her own self had a front-row seat to the ending of the snafu. Seeing as how Oklahoma's recount was the last one, and Okmulgee County's the final one tallied in the state — both of which ended up in ties — Congress and the Supreme Court finally decided to settle the matter by emergency coin-flip right there in town, where the voting and counting had finally ended. Unfortunately, the official silver dollar got put in the clumsy hands of Mayor Bailey, previously known around town as "Booster," but from then on famous worldwide as "Thumbs" Bailey. Local folks were still embarrassed as if he had broke wind on TV, a second time, but so far no one had threw a hat into the upcoming Mayoral election. So there was no news to report about that, and with only about a month to go before voting day, it was unlikely there ever would be.

While mindlessly opening mail, Henryetta had unfolded a flyer printed on yellow paper: *HENRYETTA HIGH SCHOOL ALL-CLASS REUNION, Friday Night Reception in the Gym, Free Refreshments and Banjo Music.* Huh. This was her own Fifth Reunion year and... No, Gaylord dropped out of high school before he would have flunked out, so he was not an "old grad" of dear old HHS who would likely come to the reunion. On the other hand, after he won the Heisman Trophy for being the best college football player in history, the School Board hung a picture of him in the gym, along with a framed honorary diploma. Heck, the little ol' town she'd been named after was now almost famous statewide as HOTAGG — "Hometown of Troy Aikman," also a famous football player from the past, "and Gaylord Goodhart" — but as far as she knew, Gaylord had never passed its way since leaving. Teary again — this time in despair that she would likely never get to look into Gaylord's green eyes and understand what happened — Henryetta tossed the yellow flyer aside and picked up...

Huh. An over-sized, squarish envelope was addressed in fancy handwriting to her personally. It was postmarked as sent from Dallas, TX. Henryetta had a hopeful feeling it might be a card from Gaylord, and with a little heart flutter...

THE DALLAS COWBOYS
Dooley Doolittle · Owner

Are Pleased to Announce
the Wedding of
GAYLORD GOODHART, Studback
and
BILLY RAY WILLIAMS, Wideout

Halftime in the Ring of Honor · Cowboys vs. Redskins
November 15

DOOLEY WORLD
Arlington, Texas

Sponsored by Nike

Maybe because a teardrop fell onto the invitation, blurring the name of Gaylord's chosen one, Henryetta could not bring herself to truly believe that Gaylie, who would always be the love of her life, was getting married to... another.

TWO

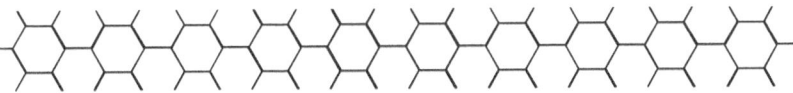

Hilde Moon Bottomly stood on a Division Street sidewalk, dismayed by changed conditions. The foundation of a two-story Victorian house, that had been a girlhood home to her, seemed to have settled into its weedy patch of red clay. Peeling whitish paint revealed brownish blotches on the building's wood facade. Moldy flower boxes sagged beneath filmy window panes that vacantly stared back at her like the uncomprehending eyes of an old woman. Though she had lived in the house for only a year following her father's retirement from the Air Force, it had felt more solid, secure and permanent than any of her family's prior quarters on or near military bases, where the incessant roar of Air Force bombers in the skies overhead made the ground shake. For decades since the demise of her parents, she had retained ownership of the property from afar, with a vague notion in mind of someday returning to the only place on earth where she had felt at least partially rooted. Not until today, however, after an absence of fifty years, had she again set foot in the small Oklahoma town called Henryetta.

Hilde—who always wore pantsuits, and was otherwise a virtual Hillary Rodham Clinton doppelganger, people said—waddled to the front door, paused with a sigh, and entered the house with a mixed sense of nostalgia and regret. Like Hillary Clinton, she too had gone east for college—to Wellesley, in Massachusetts—then on to an eastern law school. Like Hillary, she too had thereafter dedicated herself to public service—for twenty-five years as a lawyer at HUD, the federal Department of Housing and Urban Development, and for fifteen years afterward as a political appointee at the Internal Revenue Service. And like Hillary, she too had tagged along in the wake of a loose-swinging dick—namely William "Buddy" Moon—as the "silent partner" in their domestic enterprise, never getting the recognition she deserved.

She, not Buddy, had been both the brains and brawn behind their "co-founding" of the Homes Sweet Homes Foundation, a lucrative non-profit organization dedicated to building affordable housing for the less fortunate low-income members of society, and collecting fees in the process of doing good deeds. She, not Buddy, had worked the inside angles for obtaining federal and philanthropic funding. She, not Buddy, had got calluses on her knees from hour upon hour upon hour of soliciting donations from wealthy men, while he walked the other side of the street. All Buddy had brought into their marital venture was his so-called "likability," a line of BS, and regular contributions of STDs from tawdry female "donors."

Muttering a stream of curses beneath her breath, Hilde climbed a flight of bare wood stairs toward the bedroom where once upon a time she had dreamed of... "Damnit!" If only she had returned to this small Oklahoma town years ago for, say, her parents' funerals, she might have stayed here, and might have bloomed where she was planted, so to speak. She, not that moronic door-to-door salesman, Virgil Carter, might have become involved in local electoral politics. She, not that misogynistic asshole, Carter, might have said or done something to catch the attention of the national media. She, not that stupid bastard, might have been tapped for the Vice-Presidential slot on the Democratic Party ticket. And now, four years later, she—not that conniving bitch, Hillary Clinton—could have been the odds-on front runner to be the first woman elected President of the United States!

At the top of the stairs, breathless, Hilde steadied herself before entering the bedroom, where once upon a time she had dreamed of growing a... uh, of growing up to be a man. Inside the bedroom, an opened book lay upon a table, *The Squab/1965*. No doubt her classmate and professional colleague, Maude Rouser—who rented the Division Street house—had left their high school yearbook there for her. Rather than make her own annual trip to Washington, Maude had pleaded for Hilde to help her with some small town political issues faced by the local Homes Sweet Homes franchise, and while she was in town, make an appearance at their Fiftieth Henryetta High School Reunion. Truth be told, Hilde had found it a convenient time to be absent from Washington for a few days. An HSH lawyer had informed her that a minor congressional committee was asking silly questions about potential conflicts of interest during her periods of pubic service at HUD and the IRS. So she'd come to Maude's rescue as requested, but had made no commitment to attend the reunion.

Looking down at a page in the yearbook, Hilde—now blonde and wearing blue contact lenses—hardly recognized the brown-haired, brown-eyed, round-faced, round-shouldered girl staring back at her through round horn-rimmed glasses... properly identified, thankfully, as **HILDEGARD BOTTOMLY** and by her correct nickname, *Little Beaver*... not by the mean spirited *"Hilde-lard-Bottomly"* or equally hurtful, *"Zafty."* She was also thankful to be reminded that the cartoon beneath her picture showed an Indian youth named Little Beaver—mascot of her father's unit of World War II bombardiers—and not a certain other also cartoonish character with which she had sometimes been cruelly identified. That "Hilda" was a famous so-called pin-up girl, always shown as futilely struggling to free herself from cords, wires, dog leashes and other entanglements that pulled at her scanty clothes. The boys in her class had found her displayed on a calendar stuck to the wall of an auto repair shop, from which they had learned that the word *zaftig* was an adjective, that when applied to a female meant "having a full rounded figure." But Hilde too had learned something from the experience, namely that moronic males, and females too, tended to think blue-eyed blondes were attractive.

Scanning the remainder of her half-page in the Seniors section of *The Squab… National Honor Society*… Girls Bathroom Monitor… Young Republican Bombardiers for Goldwater, Founder… Dicksy Chix Barbershop Quartet… Fighting Hens Tuba Queen (Honorable Mention)… Debate Club… Student Council… Most Likely to…* Missing was correct mention of what should have been her crowning achievement, but… Hilde blotted out a few bits of misinformation with black ink from a felt-tipped pen. For having been a "Fighting Henryetta Hen" only one year, her official high school *curriculum vitae* was impressive enough; certainly she had no reason to feel embarrassed by anything in her youthful past. Perhaps she would attend the class reunion after all, and…

For dear old HHS, we'll yell and yell and yell, sang a familiar deep voice from behind her. *And fight, fight, fight to score…*

Hilde turned to see Maude Rouser remove a gray wig from her head of thinning reddish hair, then drop her old-fashioned house dress to the floor; shedding, as it were, the persona of kindly old "Aunt Maude" that she affected for local Homes

Sweet Homes fund raising and promotional purposes. In pink peddle-pushers, neon-orange tank top — emblazoned *Tremble! Tremble! The Bitches Are Loose!* — but still wearing granny glasses, Maude came to the table and began to thumb yearbook pages. "Remember that cute little cheerleader, Cissy Golightly?" she said. "Wait'll you see what she looks like now: a shrunken, little old man."

"Oh yes, Cissy Golightly was voted 'Most Likely to Get Knocked Up' before end of the school year," said Hilde, "and as I recall... Oh my God," she then said, reaching across Maude to halt her friend's thumbing. A photo of a young Elvis impersonator... with long, though yellow swept-back hair and a puckered smirk on his bow-shaped lips... **JONATHAN HENRY**... nicknamed *Stinky*. Nothing was listed below the picture on his Senior page except ***Most Likely to End Up Broke***. Both Hilde and Maude looked up from the page. Their eyes met. Without a word passing between them, both began to howl with laughter, though the incident they jointly recalled was for Hilde a somewhat bitter-sweet memory.

Jonathan Henry, a spoiled though not so little rich kid, had recently been kicked out of reform school — the so-called Oklahoma Military Academy — and had returned to Henryetta High for his Senior year. Feeling their shared friendless status was something they had in common, Hilde had summoned up the nerve to ask him to be her date to a Sadie Hawkins Day dance in the high school gym. "You?!" he'd said, looking down at her with arched eyebrows and pursed lips. "You and me?" he said, obviously incredulous of the possibility of the two of them having a date. "Fat chance," he'd said, with his chronic smirk. "Very fat chance! And by the way, you're also stupid."

After months of plotting revenge with Maude... Hilde,

mortified but still convulsed in hysterical laughter, recalled "doing her business" into a brown paper bag, then wedging the Christmas present into the springs under the driver's seat of Jonathan's shiny new red Mustang convertible. "He couldn't get a second date with anyone all Spring!" Maude howled, "and had to steal his daddy's big Cadillac to get Cissy to let him escort her to the prom. If not for the Caddy's roomy back seat, he might never have had reason to believe he was the one who knocked her up! Ha, ha, ha, ha, ha, ha...

"They got divorced after about a year together," Maude reported, drying her eyes with a hankie. "And since then, Stinky has been married and divorced at least six times, mainly to women from out of town, two from out of the country."

"Good," said Hilde, with a vicious smile, spitefully gratified to have played a role in fulfilling the fates predicted for both Cissy Golightly and Jonathan Henry. With multiple divorces in his past... "Alas, no," said Maude, reading her thoughts, "Stinky is reputed to be an artful master at negotiating pre-nup 'deals'. The Jonathan — that's what people call him now — inherited the old Bunkhouse Motel on Main Street that backs up to the town jail, and franchised the corny brand in every state on this side of the Mississippi. You can't drive fifty miles on a western interstate highway without a dozen billboards inviting you to 'Kick the bullshit off your boots and stay a spell' at a JHA Bunkhouse Motel."

That settled it. With any possibility of her making an appearance at the high school reunion now out of the question, Hilde slammed the yearbook shut. "Oh please, at least come to tomorrow night's reception," Maude begged. "You'll like seeing how badly all the in-crowd girls have aged. It would be good for you to meet Mayor Bailey in a relaxed social setting, where you can turn on your charm. And the other Dicksy Chix and I, we want to make fun of the high school fight song, for old times' sake." *Oh, when those Golden Knights all fall in line*, Maude sang in her bass voice, *we're gonna cheer our team and yell, yell, yell/ And fight, fight, fight for evermore/ The Golden Knights will lose for sure/ For dear old HHS…*

"Golden Knights?"

"Oh yeah, the boys got the school mascot changed back in 1989. They said a 'Fighting Hens' football team was sissified, even though boys from other towns, and girls, called them 'Fighting Peckers'."

Hilde fumed. "Why was I not informed of this… this setback in the War on Women right here in my own hometown?" she sputtered. "Maude! Gird your loins and prepare for battle. Once more, Dicksy Chix must lock arms and march into the breach!"

Oh, when those Fighting Hens all fall in line/ For old HHS we'll yell, yell, yell / And fight, fight, fight…

THREE

Alone at the bar of the P's-n-Q's pool hall and quaint cafe, barely holding back tears from spilling into a mug of beer, Henryetta again asked herself: Why should she care that Gaylord Goodhart was getting married? Yes, Gaylord and she had gone at it steady during one of their teen years in high school. But that was probably just what they called puberty hormones at work. It was more her mother, Wynona Sue, who had been eager as a new bride for them to get hitched soon as they graduated. She her own self on the other hand… Henryetta's eyes dried up and got hot as fever. No, it was her mother who was to blame for what happened. When Wynona Sue got fearful of Gaylie going off to college to play football, she took up with his daddy, Coach Goodhart, which was about as weird as double-dating in a back seat for Gaylord and her. And after Coach drove the school bus into a ditch, with Wynona Sue in the back seat, naked… Well, things were never the same between either couple, and not long afterward Gaylord and his daddy left town.

"Well, I declare," said her mother, suddenly at Henryetta's side, come from work at The Best Little Hair House in Town. "What in tarnation is so all-fired important that I had to take Miz Parker's head out of the oven before it was done?" Her mother took no notice of the tears that started running down Henryetta's face. Instead, after picking up the fancy wedding invitation off the bar, "Well, I _do_ declare," she said. "Gaylord

Goodhart… Halftime in a Ring of Honor… at Dooley World! That's the big ol' stadium down in Dallas where Dolly Parton, wearing a low-cut star-spangled dress when they played that *Taps* song 'stead of the national anthem and… His daddy, Cecil, will be there, and I don't have a thing to wear!"

Henryetta's tears again dried up. "As I recall, that's just the way Coach Goodhart likes you," she said to her mother. "Maybe you two can get yourselves arrested again, and your names put in the paper!"

"Why, Henryetta Hebert, how could you say such a hurtful thing? You know very well that was an elopement accident. I was changing into a wedding dress on our way to Fort Smith: floor-length of course, plus white satin top with a scooped neckline and almost-cultured pearl-studded bodice that I never got to…" With her own eyes welled up with tears, Wynona Sue raised a finger to signal the bartender to bring a glass of white wine. Henryetta bit her tongue. What she knew very well was that her mother had put a curse on her at birth. By naming her only child after the little ol' town of Henryetta, Oklahoma — spelled with a y where an i should have been put — Wynona Sue had tried to tie her down there by apron strings. That was also the reason she took up with Gaylord's daddy, Henryetta had come to realize, and the same reason she had chased one man after another through the years. After being abandoned as a young mother, Wynona Sue was scared of being left all alone. They had covered the subject a hundred times before, so there was no need to…

"Henryetta, I have told you a hundred times: It was a typo on your birth certificate," said her mother, reading Henryetta's mind like she'd always been able to do. "I was too upset at the time to get it fixed, what with your no-account Cajun daddy run off and me left holding the sack."

"Yeah, but two or three other times, after two or three Friendly Creature highballs, you let slip the truth," said Henryetta, despite herself. "You said that if my no-account Cajun daddy had been content to be plain ol' 'Hinry Heeburt' 'stead of 'Ahn-REE Aybear', he never would have had the nerve to chase after that rich 'whore' in Tulsa, and she never would have let him ketch her."

Wynona Sue pushed her glass of white wine away and changed her order to a Friendly Creature highball. "People would have called you 'Ahn-REE-etta'," she said, "which sounds almost like 'Orneryetta'. You might have took up Cajun voodoo ways like your Grandma Hebert and… Anyway, it wouldn't have made any difference," she said, back to studying the wedding invitation. "If Gaylord's full-blooded Indian mama had not run off when he was a toddler; if she had sacrificed her own happiness to raise him right, like other mothers do, she would have took him into the woods to see if he came back with a bow-and-arrow or a doll, or both. Gaylord would have known from the start he was what his mother's people call 'two-spirited'. You might have been able to ketch him, but you never would have had what it took to keep him hitched to a bedstead post."

Henryetta had to admit to her own self that what her mother said was likely true enough. Though Gaylord was not exactly dumb, he had always been on the simple-minded side about "birds-and-bees" sorts of things, she recalled. Probably Gaylie his own self didn't know he was gay until he went off to the Texas State Penitentiary to play bigtime prison football for the TSP Chain Gang, where he was Billy Ray Williams' cellmate and teammate. On the other hand, if he had stayed in town and finished high school before ending up over at Murray State University—with Billy Ray 'stead of her—he might have kept on the hetero side of his "two-spirited" inclinations. On the other other hand... Noticing that tears were now running down Wynona Sue's face like sweat on a chilled mug of beer, Henryetta felt bad for making her mother feel guilty. "Oh well, I reckon it's all turned out for the best," she said, semi-sincerely.

"Not for me," said her mother. "Henryetta, do you happen to know if Cecil Goodhart is currently single?"

Dang it! If her boss at the *Weekly Herald* newspaper, Mr. Harold Mixon, had not rushed into the P's-n-'Q's right then, Henryetta would have told her self-central mother that by now such a fine upstanding man as Coach Goodhart was bound to have kept his eye on the road—'stead of the rearview mirror—and eloped with someone sober and un-naked, but... "Henryetta, I'm glad I found you," said Mr. Harold. "I've heard late-breaking news: Gaylord Goodhart is going to enter into wedlock with... another Dallas Cowboy... who is likely to also be... male. And seein' as how he was once, uh, your young man, I wanted to tell you... Oh, how do, Miz Hebert," Mr. Harold said to her mother, before asking about Wynona Sue's health, and hearing about it.

Henryetta was touched that her boss—who usually didn't give a hoot-nor-holler about sports world news—had brought a shoulder for her to cry on, but... "Henryetta, national news media will be wanting background, and quotes about Gaylord's hometown days," Mr. Harold said, "so you need to write-up a story from your unique personal perspective."

Feeling untouched, Henryetta gave up on other peoples' shoulders and re-commenced to drown her sorrow in *Hairy Dog Home Brew.*

"We'll be known all over the country as the 'Hometown of Gaylord Goodhart'," Mr. Harold continued. "The young man is a hero to people around here, and, uh, they say his 'bride' is also from Oklahoma."

Henryetta like to spit out a mouthful of beer. "How do you know Gaylord his own self is not gonna be the 'bride'?" she said, sarcastically. "He's 'two-spirited', ya know," she said to her boss, but with a sideways glare at her mother. "You think local folks are ready to admire their hero in a long white dress, with scooped neckline and pearl-studded bodice?"

"No! That would be a disgrace!" said Wynona Sue, seeming also put-off by the very thought of such an unsightly spectacle. "The new look for this Fall's brides is loose-fittin' Arabian bloomers, with flowing scarves hangin' from head to foot, all silk and all white of course."

"Hmmm," Mr. Harold hmmed. "And there will be a picture when the big event happens, I suppose. I hadn't thought through the 'optics' of the story, and the possible side effects of... Henryetta, get right on this before big city tabloids start spreading sensational gossip," said her boss, "and, uh, keep it personal, with not too much about the town. Don't get into any girly talk about bodices or flowing scarves."

"Say we would be happy to send down a hometown bridesmaid," said her mother. "And write down this quote, Henryetta: 'As someone who, but for a tragic accident, was almost related to Gaylord by unsame-sex-marriage—as both step-mother and mother-in-law—I would be honored to get a new dress myself and serve at the big event in Dallas."

Henryetta burst into bawling. "There, there, there," said Mr. Harold, backing toward a fire exit. "Now, now, now," said Wynona Sue, getting off her barstool to pat her on the back. "Henryetta, it's been years since Gaylord Goodhart handed you the mitten. I know it hurts, honey, but you need to get over that two-spirited boy and go on down the... the... "

Henryetta got off her own barstool and commenced to pat her bawling mother on the back. "There, there, there... "

"You're the lucky one, Henryetta," said Wynona Sue, sobbing on her shoulder. "You don't have to see the other <u>woman</u> march down the aisle in Arabian silk bloomers."

As was occasionally the case, Henryetta reckoned that her mother, Wynona Sue, might have got it about half right.

FOUR

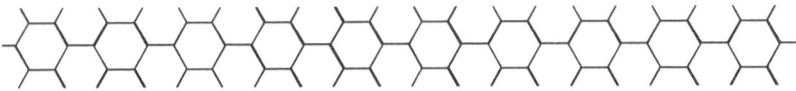

From a Lazy-Boy recliner across from a TV, Mayor Buford P. Bailey watched an ancient Roman emperor continue to make life-or-death decisions from a stadium box seat, while he himself tried to decide what positions to take in his campaign for re-election. After decades of involvement in local politics dating back to elementary school contests for student council positions, four years ago he had sniffed inklings of a calling to higher office. But a single digital miscue... *Hail, Caesar! Thumbs up, or thumbs down?...* had then very nearly cost him his political life. Though bloodied by unfavorable press coverage, not to mention unfair rock-throwing, after reading an inspirational book by former President Richard Nixon and binge-watching a DVD movie about the ups and downs of the Roman Empire, he had soldiered on with promotion of ambitious programs for the town's economic development. And gradually had regained his good name, "Booster" Bailey. Now he grinned with satisfaction, as always, when the on-screen emperor raised two thumbs of approval for a gladiator's gritty performance in the arena.

Unfortunately, however, all of Buford's economic development initiatives — through no fault of his own — had come a cropper: Lake Henryetta, the town's reservoir of drinking water, had proved to be insufficiently infused with insufficiently miraculous nitrous oxide to guarantee eternal human life, making export of the liquid commodity pointless and unprofitable. Later, after extending city limits miles westward to accommodate a municipal golf course, and town dump, a methane gas fire in the dump had forced cancellation of a nationally televised golf tournament at the publicly funded Hogback Hot Links. Default on bond payments and loss of the golf course land had followed. Otherwise, construction of high-class Spanish mansions would have transformed the hogback on the new west side of town into a veritable "Pebble Beach of Oklahoma." Now the town was broke, unable even to fill the many pot holes in its streets. Now only uneconomic development was on the table, put there by that pesky "Aunt Maude" and the so-called Homes Sweet Homes Association, who wanted to build affordable housing for poor people instead of unaffordable Spanish mansions for rich folks who could charge things to credit cards and pay local sales taxes.

Hail, Caesar! Thumbs up, or thumbs down?

Again grinning, Buford extended his arms toward the TV screen and enthusiastically turned two thumbs down, fully in agreement with the Roman emperor's decision. The dark-skinned so-called "Amazonian" woman, no doubt an illegal immigrant from South America, had nearly castrated her male opponent with a low blow delivered by a long, sharp sword.

Though he was a sitting Mayor, and unopposed in the upcoming election—perhaps because the municipal seat was mainly ceremonial, barely salaried, and largely thankless—Buford planned to launch an aggressive campaign for a third term. A landslide victory might put him back in the national spotlight and lead to a bigger seat. To achieve such a triumph, however, would be hard to pull off in the current political environment of public disgust for politicians. With only five weeks remaining 'til Election Day, time was short for coming up with a clever slogan and eye-catching campaign sign design, along with generous political contributions, of course, mainly in the form of supporters' permission to place the signs on their property. And, dang it, he needed an issue—along with a position on an issue—to fire up the uninformed, unengaged masses and inspire high voter turn-out. But what issue? What might people care about that didn't amount to a government hand-out?

Having recently watched hours of nightly cable news shows and studied public opinion polls in *USA Today*, Buford now referred to a list of possible planks of a campaign platform he had jotted down:

Did "Black Lives Matter"? Hmmm... *Hail Caesar! Thumbs up, or thumbs down?* No, he decided, black lives didn't matter, at least not much; not in Henryetta, Oklahoma. The town was populated by only a handful of African-Americans—all Democrats, no doubt—and none likely to vote for anything other than a full-course free lunch.

Hmmm, what about the 'Fight Against Global Warming"? But no, in the aftermath of a recent lawsuit by farmers and ranchers against Oklahoma cities and towns for causing the heat problem, local citizens were all for burning fossil fuels to change the climate.

So-called "Economic Justice"? Nope, there was no local income inequality to speak of. About everyone in town was equally broke. No doubt a large majority of residents would be strongly in favor of becoming underserving "havers" and let others remain deserving "have-nots," but no one would believe that was possible anymore.

As for the issue of "Illegal Immigration Reform"... *Hail, Caesar! Thumbs up, or thumbs down?*

Startled by loud banging on the front door of his Trudgeon Street bungalow, Buford pulled a lever to launch himself from the Lazy-Boy. At the door... "Sorry to barge in on you at home, Booster," said—of all people—Harold Mixon himself, owner, publisher and editor-in-chief of the *Weekly Herald*. "The town's got a doozy of an issue on its hands," the so-called shaper of local public opinion reported, before plopping himself down in Buford's recliner. "I'm afraid you're gonna have to at least postpone putting up at least one of those statues on Main Street," he said, wiping his brow with a handkerchief. "Probably another dumb idea of yours to begin with. You know, we used to have that statue of a World War I 'Doughboy' out there, and even he became a nuisance, which was a small hill o' beans compared to what's sure to happen if... "

Dang it! The fancy-pants editor, who had gone out of state to a four-year college, was talking about Buford's current pet project: placement of life-size statues of the town's two most famous homegrown heroes—football players, Troy Aikman and Gaylord Goodhart—in the center of two Main Street intersections. Aikman, a legendary Dallas Cowboy from the past, was to go at 6th Street and Main, where the old Doughboy used to stand. Goodhart, a current Cowboy star player, was to be put at 4th and Main. And at 5th Street, midway between the two sculpted heroes, two real-life leather footballs hanging on a cable strung across Main Street would look like they had been thrown or kicked from one Cowboy to the other. The tableau—that's what the new owner of the Dallas team, Mr. Doolittle, called it: a French tableau—was a duplicate of one he himself was fixing to erect in his big stadium down in Texas, soon as corporate sponsors paid to put advertising on the artwork.

"Hold your water, Harold," Buford took delight in saying to the long-winded word writer. "The statues are only French plaster models for metal sculptures to be unveiled at a Ring of

Honor ceremony in Dallas this Fall. I got 'em at no cost to the town. A benefactor, Mr. Doolittle, gets only a tax deduction for the heroes. And the footballs... "

"It's not an issue of cost," Mixon said, ejecting himself out of the Lazy-Boy. "Don't you keep up with things, Booster? Goodhart is about to get married, to a Dallas teammate, for cryin' out loud!"

Though a confirmed, lifelong bachelor himself, Buford failed to see why Gaylord Goodhart's marital inclination would be cause for...

"It'll be a so-called same-sex 'Ring of Honor' ceremony, Buford. The plaster statue of Goodhart may show up here with him wearing a... We can't have young school children looking up a hero's dress... And those balls hanging in the air... It's an indecent tableau, suited for Paris, France or Dallas, Texas maybe, but not for our town!"

"School kids donated lunch money for those balls, Harold; they didn't cost the town a penny. They've already been partially inflated and hung. No one has made an issue of them. It's you, Harold, who haven't been keeping up with flux!"

"You're the Mayor," Mister SmartyPants admitted, "at least for now, but I'm warning you, Buford, I may have to write one of my powerful **From Where I Sit** editorials on the subject and put it on the front page of the paper."

After the old, over-the-hill newspaper man had stormed out, Buford plopped himself back into the Lazy-Boy, only slightly worried. Harold Mixon's front page editorials regularly appeared—under a photo of a famous statue of a naked man, sitting on what looked like a commode, with one elbow on his knee, resting his head in a hand—and were made fun of by almost everyone in town. Nevertheless, back to mulling possible campaign issues, he jotted on his list: *Football Player Erections and Hanging Balls?*

Hail, Caesar! Thumbs up, or thumbs down?

FIVE

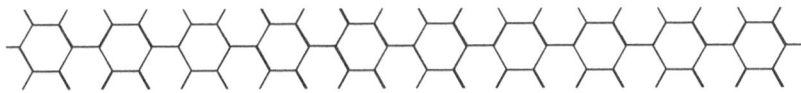

Mr. Harold's grandson needed to use the *Weekly Herald's* laptop word processor for an online spelling bee, and Henryetta had found that at the office—with her boss settin' right behind her, mumbling about one of his front page **From Where I Sit** editorials— she couldn't get in the mood to write a story about Gaylord "from her unique personal perspective." So at a pink formica dinette table in her singles-only Shangri-La apartment, she took a sharp pencil in hand and began to scribble on a legal-size yellow pad: *HENRYETTA, OK: This little dot at the intersection of the Indian Nation Parkway and Interstate 40 was mainly known as HOTA—Hometown of Troy Aikman—when Gaylord Goodhart arrived. He was already seventeen years of age and, abandoned as a toddler by his Native American mother, had been raised in various other towns by his daddy, Cecil Goodhart, who was the new high school football coach. Without being asked about his own preference, Gaylord's daddy had put a football in his son's crib—long before high school—and pushed him toward getting a scholarship to play ball at the University of Texas, then go on to be an All-Pro studback for the Dallas Cowboys. But Gaylord his own self had his heart set on...*

Henryetta put down the pencil, leaned back in her chair, and recalled the first time she set eyes on Gaylord Goodhart: Being about half Indian, he was dark skinned; half somethin else, green-eyed; and all in all, the prettiest boy, or girl, in school.

He wasn't dumb, it wasn't that he didn't understand the Chinese signal boards his daddy flashed at him during football practices and games; he just couldn't seem to concentrate his mind. Looking toward the sideline, Gaylord's attention was inclined to focus on the even more complicated routines of the all-girl cheerleading squad. Off the field, he was too shy to flirt back at the big-breasted pep girls. Instead, for some reason Henryetta had never quite understood, he took to her, or at least acted like it some of the time.

Gaylord his own self dreamed of going down to College Station after high school, to play football for Texas A&M and lead cheers for the Aggie corps of cadets, but... Henryetta paused to sharpen her pencil, while deciding how to put it delicately, and not embarrass her mother, Wynona Sue. *His daddy, Coach Goodhart, got fired before the start of Gaylord's Senior year, for being at the wheel of a school bus bound for Arkansas that ended up in a ditch. Gaylord started drinking beer and smoking pot, sometimes right on school grounds. He got into fights on and off the field. He didn't have a good year at playing football, didn't make a single passing grade in class, and didn't get scholarship offers from any college. Though he seemed not to care, his heart was no doubt broke by...*

To get a grip on her own heart, Henryetta put down the sharp pencil. Her mother, Wynona Sue, had liked Gaylord a lot, and the feeling was mutual. All Spring and into the Summer before their Senior year, he was all the time coming over to her house on Trudgeon Street, and didn't seem to mind Wynona Sue staying up with them to watch a TV show, or just talk. Having never known his own mama, he had never had anyone stroke his cheek and tell him everything was going to be alright.

"Gaylie, honey, you don't wanna be a soldier, do you?" Wynona Sue would say. "You don't want to march off with a gun on your shoulder and never come back home."

"No ma'am," he would answer, "I'd never want to shoot at nobody."

"Well, that's what they'd make you do down at that Texas A&M: put you in that corps of cadets, either that or the band. I saw 'em on television one time, marching around on a football field. Now, wouldn't you druther stay here on the sideline, where it's safe."

"Yes ma'am, I don't want to get shot at neither. But I sure enough would like to go down there and… "

"You just stay right here," Wynona Sue would say, maybe with a pat to Gaylord's knee as she got up from the divan. "After you get through playin' that football, you can he'p your daddy coach it, and take over from him one of these days. More pie, honey?"

When Wynona Sue and Coach Goodhart started keeping company with one another, Gaylord and she began to drift apart, Henryetta now sadly recalled. After the "elopement accident" happened, he wouldn't touch her like he did before, and she her own self was not much interested in any serious "tickling" neither. But she still loved him, and later realized…

The thing that broke Gaylord's heart was Texas A&M dropping out of playing football, Henryetta wrote, *which turned out to be just the start of bigtime college ball's collapse everywhere and the rise of bigtime prison football in its place. By the time Gaylord got kicked out of the army and enrolled in Murray State University over in Tishomingo, the no-account Cantwell brothers, A.C and D.C — rival head coaches of the the Texas Chain Gang and Oklahoma Wild Bunch — had started playing dirty tricks to "recruit" him. A no-account District Attorney over in Tishomingo charged Gaylie with helping another recruit have his way with a barroom floozy. About to be found guilty of that crime, he ran away, but then got charged with murdering his*

own daddy, Coach Cecil Goodhart, in Texas waters of Lake Texoma.
Clear as a widow woman's bedroom windows, the rape charge was
false, but...

Recalling the gory details of what happened, Henryetta got
up from her writing and commenced to pace. A fisherman in a
boat said he saw another fella in the same area of Lake Texoma,
doing what he thought was chumming—throwing chunks of
bait into the water to attract fish—'cept he never got around to
wetting a line. He just chummed. And when the two of them
steered their boats into a marina on the Texas side of the lake,
the chummer—later identified as Gaylord—was drenched in
blood. A thumb found on the bow of his boat was also later
identified, as none other than the remains of his daddy, Coach
Cecil. And in open court, Gaylord his own self admitted not
only to the killing, but also to chopping off his daddy's fingers,
toes and pecker, pushing his face into the boat's propellor, and
eating his brains on a cheese sandwich. Needless to say...

After agreeing not to appeal his death sentence, which guaranteed
he would not serve longer than the five years allowed for bigtime
prison football eligibility, Gaylord became a super-star for the Texas
Chain Gang. The Texas State Penitentiary had bought the abandoned
Texas A&M stadium by then, and their team became real popular as
sort of the new Aggies. In addition to running, passing, and kicking
up and down the field, Gaylord led complicated cheers of the corps of
cadets, just like he had dreamed of doing. But then someone spotted a
Chain Gang fan in the stands, wearing a rainbow wig, yelling and
screaming like, well, like a Texas Aggie, while holding up a "We're
Number 1" foam finger with one hand, and missing a thumb off the
other.

Henryetta went on to write about how Gaylord got kicked
out of Texas after his undead daddy's recruiting scandal was

discovered; and how he got cleared of rape charges in Oklahoma after someone mislaid the jury verdict that had been jotted on a scrap of paper. Briefly, she recounted how Gaylord—and a certain unnamed wideout—led the Murray State Alfalfa Bills to a national championship in what turned out to be the last bigtime college football season ever played. Then, sure as crickets followed August drought that her piece would have no chance of winning one of those Pulitzer Prizes for good journalism, she folded three pages of legal-size yellow paper and headed for the *Weekly Herald* office.

Mr. Harold started scanning what she wrote, saying "hmm" about one thing or another that he read. With a final hmm, he looked up, took off his reader glasses, and said: "The last part wanders out of town and beyond your personal unique perspective, Henryetta, and as for the first part... "

"I reckon it was when Gaylord went to prison down in Texas that he got, uh, close to Billy Ray," she argued. "It must have been lonely for him to be cooped up down there and... "

"Oh, okay, I see your point," her boss said. "Prisons breed that sort of unnatural behavior, and your young man was long gone from town and your wholesome feminine influence by then. But I don't like this suggestion in the first part about him coming under the influence of cheerleading while he was here. All our high school pep squads have always been girls. What's lacking is... "

"Like I said, Mr. Harold, Gaylie is half Indian, on his mama's side. I reckon he was what they call two-spirited at birth. It was his daddy who put a football in his crib. I reckon he was naturally inclined to 'cheerleadin' from the day he was born."

"No, it's a lifestyle choice," her boss argued, "made mainly by young people these days to get attention, and companionship.

Uh, less attractive gals who can't get a boyfriend, and nerdy boys who can't get a date with a girl, sometimes resort to... Fine, if Lucy loves Lucy, let 'em carry on however they want to, but as for marriage... "

"Gaylie's not unenjoyable to look at. He could have gone with any girl in town. The only thing noticeably 'queer' about him was that he chose me."

But Mr. Harold had already about finished writing his front page editorial and she could see his head was set like sidewalk cement on the subject of Gaylord and his same-sex marriage. He argued that one man-one woman wedlock was a cornerstone of western civilization, going back thousands of years, and had never had much to do with whether "John loved Lucy, or vice versa," until lonely English women started writing novel books for other lonely women to read. To her boss, the fact that ordinary opposite-sex marriage had not worked out for a lot of guys and gals — "as gay people point out, to claim it's no big deal"—was a bogus argument against traditional wedlock. "How come they call their mates 'husbands' and 'wives'?" he asked. "How come they have to call their unions 'marriage'? Isn't it telling," he said, "that with so many mis-called liberals trying to eliminate 'hateful' gender identity, the very ones in relationships where gender 'discrimination' is most absent try to re-create the difference."

As her usually wide-minded boss went on sputtering, Henryetta realized that what had got him so het up was the thought of being called a bigot—"wrongfully accused of hating someone"—for not taking right away to a revolutionary notion that had been suddenly sprung on normal folks out of nowhere.

"Have you ever looked up the definition of bigotry, Henryetta?" he asked. "Bigotry is intolerance toward those who hold opinions different from your own. So I say it's the vocal minority of a single uneducated, narcissistic generation who are themselves blindly bigoted in their trendy, politically correct rejection of the sum total of human wisdom accumulated over ages. I don't care if Gaylord Goodhart and his boyfriend want to dress-up for a spectacle in a football stadium, and go play house together, but I am dead set against a statue being put up in the middle of Main Street, showing a local hero in a... "

"Mr. Harold, when I made that crack at the P's-n-Q's bar about Gaylord being a 'bride' and wearing a dress, I was just being spiteful," Henryetta confessed, but her boss had gone back to perusing her article and saying hmmm. "Yeah, this part is okay as far as it goes," he said again, without looking up. "But I would like for you to make it clearer that this young man had a perfectly normal life in our perfectly normal town," he said, drooping his head down more, and his voice. "You were a pretty young thing, Henryetta," he mumbled, "and, well, there must have been some sparkin' goin' on between you two out by Possum Pond, so... "

"What did you say? I can't hardly hear you, Mr. Harold."

Her boss looked up with a reddish face, and in a semi-whisper: "Henryetta, I think readers would like to know, and need to know, that you and your young man — Gaylord Goodhart — had a perfectly normal relationship when you were both in high school, and that he showed no signs of becoming what they call 'gay' when he left town."

Henryetta took back the yellow sheets of paper her boss stuck out to her. Truth be told, she had begun to have a notion that it might have been somethin' about her own not so feminine wholesome self that had pushed Gaylord in an "unnatural" direction, but she dang sure didn't want to write about it in a newspaper.

SIX

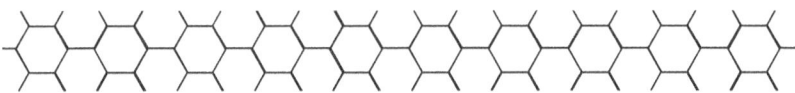

In the lobby of the Bunkhouse Motel on Main Street in downtown Henryetta, Jonathan Henry paused to check his appearance—not as reflected in a mirror—as represented by a somewhat dated, life-size plastic statue, duplicates of which graced the lobbies of the entire interstate chain of branded *JAH Bunkhouses*. "Not bad," he said aloud to himself, fluffing a comb-over of longish hair, now slightly less yellow than in the 1990 sculpture that—when operational—opened its mouth and delivered a recorded message in his own voice. "In fact, incredibly fantastic for a living legend of my age," he confirmed to himself, before reluctantly turning away from his likeness. "Tonto!" he shouted, in response to which a small darkish-skinned man appeared, looking downright dwarfish in stature compared the living legend, who at over six-feet in height and considerably bulkier than in the plastic depiction, was often self-described as a big man, a very big man, and rich, very rich. "Hi-yo, Silver!" he bellowed, ambling past his attendant and out the motel's swinging double-doors.

A large silver SUV—adorned with a longhorn hood ornament and plastered with JAH monograms—awaited him at the curb with an open, oversized rear door and commodious back seat upholstered in cowhide. With Tonto at the wheel, off they went to "ride fence"—"The Jonathan's" self-appointed daily task of inspecting and assigning monetary value to his local and sub-regional real estate holdings.

Though it was already past seven, he noted that his hardware store tenant was not yet open for business. And yet the old proprietor, a disabled veteran who could roll if not walk, constantly complained that the store's sales volume was insufficient to support regular semi-annual rent increases. Farther east on Main Street, near the railroad tracks, he saw that another of his prime commercial properties was not only still not generating sales, but was still boarded-up, due to an ongoing legal dispute about the collapsed roof that the tenant expected him, the building owner, to repair at his own expense. Nearby, a cluster of partly abandoned industrial buildings more positively showed increased ripeness for cheap acquisition and demolition, but there was still no sure profit in the deal unless and until local and state officials approved his plan to develop the site as a high-class nuclear waste facility. No wonder the local economy was in the tank. While he himself was really, really smart, politicians — especially the town Mayor, that baldheaded doofus, Bailey — were incredibly stupid.

In the countryside north of town, riding fence around thousands of acres he'd assembled by inheritance and foreclosure, Jonathan next saw that neither had the value of anything out there improved overnight. The government no longer paid millions of dollars in subsidies for him to not grow crops, and workers willing to till the red clay were not to be found at anything less than a so-called living wage. As a result, his fields lay fallow and unproductive. Same for his ranch properties. His *JAH*-branded cattle ate like pigs, literally, but had developed a habit of keeling over, dead, before getting beefy enough to be slaughtered at a decent price. If not for his love of horses, shared by Asians, he would have claimed bankruptcy of his ranching export business years ago. And now even that barely trickling income stream was threatened by overly burdensome federal regulations about every little edible...

"Boss! Boss! Da plane, da plane!"

Instantly, an oxygen mask dropped from the SUV ceiling into the back seat. Jonathan's sharp-eyed driver, Tonto, made a skidding U-turn, stomped on the accelerator and sped them back toward town. In the dust behind them, "Da plane" swept low across a field of cattle, spraying nutritional supplements—almost entirely harmless to most humans—that tended to irritate Jonathan's sensitive nasal passages and sinuses. Aided by the protective mask and extra oxygen intake, he was, thankfully, only moderately stuffed-up by the time they reached the Interstate, while Tonto mildly complained of only a slight rash on the nape of his neck. Headed eastward to inspect three or four of his motels alongside various highways, however, Jonathan's entire being—not just his nose—became severely irritated. Not by harmless nutrient spray, but by covetous envy of what he saw: The so-called Creek Nation Casino, less than thirty miles from his flagship Bunkhouse!

Damnit, he was part Creek Indian on his daddy's side, but had never got a drop of skimmed cream from the casino cash cow.

Hours later, immediately after exiting the interstate back into the west side of Henryetta, Jonathan hollered at Tonto to pull over at Kellogg's Korner, a plot of ground right next to the Interstate entry ramp. An abandoned service station and auto repair garage sat on the front portion of a hundred-odd acre site that he'd had his eye on for a considerable length of time. It was owned, still, by family of one of his ex-wives, Merlene, and had been a major factor, stronger than mere carnal lust, in his courtship of her thirty-odd years ago. Back then he had yearned to build a slightly larger, new and improved Bunkhouse Motel on the site. But Merlene had proved to be a gold digger who was smarter than she looked—which wasn't saying much—and hard to deal with as an IRS agent. She had refused to throw the property into a marital pot, where he could have got at it during their divorce negotiations, and through all the years since then had held onto the plot of land out of pure-dee spite. Women were like that, he'd learned in the school of hard knocks known as marriage: You treat them nice, they break your balls.

To make the matter an even more nettlesome burr in Jonathan's longjohns, during decades of frustrated desire his dreams had become grander and grander, to the point that he now salivated, literally, at the downright erotic possibility of erecting on the site a luxurious fifteen-story tower in the theme and style of a JAH Bunkhouse, including also a pair of attached annexes: One branded a *JAH Golden Corral Casino,* the other a *JAH Kitty Kat Ranch,* upscale version of a famous Nevada brothel.

Jonathan had Tonto drive the SUV around to the back of the dilapidated Kellogg's Korner service station building, from where he saw two grown-ups stooped over in a recently plowed field, with two younguns running around nearby. One of the adults straightened up and started in Jonathan's direction. It was an offspring of his, Merlene's boy, Bart, who had lived with his mother in California until a few months ago, when he came back to Oklahoma—supposedly to visit his dear old dad—and decided to settle on Merlene's family homestead. Jonathan had tried to talk his prodigal son out of such foolishness, but like his mother, the boy seemed to be naturally contrary. Now, he didn't even put out a hand to shake when they got close enough to howdy.

"Whatcha doin' out here, boy?" Jonathan asked, while continuing to look past the stubborn thirty-something sumbitch into the plowed field behind him. "That gal of yours will get old and worn out before her time if you keep workin' her out here in the hot sun like one of those Chinaman coolees who built the railroad."

"My wife's name must have slipped your mind, old man," said his son. "It's Hermione. Her straw hat is Asian, but she's French, born and raised in Thailand. And since you asked, we're spreading fertilizer, getting the soil ready to start an organic vegetable farm and vineyard."

"Oh yeah, Frenchies, they're frisky. I was married for awhile to a gal I met in the French Quarter of New Orleans. Named Nicole, as I recall. Better keep one eye open, or that foreign wife of yours will likely wear you out, with after-hours bedroom chores, and one day leave your pants hangin' on a chair, pockets empty as her wedding vows, heh, heh." And after an awkward pause: "Boy, I'm tellin' you straight: There's no profit to be made in grapes. They're too hard to grow, birds peck 'em off the vine, or they'll rot in the sun before you can get 'em picked and made into jelly to put up in Mason jars. You'd be better off to... "

"We're going to make wine," said the boy, "label it *Hermes Herbal Nectar* and get rich, like you, or rather like that great grandpa of ours I've heard so much about: the Indian who first settled in these parts and started from scratch."

"Okay, okay," said Jonathan, throwing up his arms and smiling broadly, like an indulgent daddy surrendering to the notion that foolish youth had to be be served. "Tell ya what I'll do," he said. "I'll swap, straight up, a quarter-section of prime farming land north of town—settled by Great Grandpa Hugh more than a hundred years ago—for clear title to this piece of dirt here...

to give you and the wife a chance to plant something where it might have a chance to grow," he added, with a wider smile, "and to keep the best acreage of Great Grandpa's original spread in the Henry family. Whatta you say to that, young man?"

With a thoughtful expression on his face, the boy swiveled his body to look back on the field behind him, then re-swiveled. "No, but thanks anyway," he said. "This old service station building... I know it's not much, but... We're living in it now, and later we'll be able to use it for crushing grapes and... "

"Okay, tell ya what: I'll throw in a slightly used double-wide mobile house, complete with redwood deck, and... What the hell, call me crazy. To sweeten the deal, I'll pony up an extra-large aluminum watering trough you can use as a hot tub for crushing grapes. Your ma and I used to enjoy doing almost that very thing on occasion. How 'bout it?"

His son again looked back at the field, maybe also to the wife and younguns, but... He turned again and said, "Nah, thanks anyway, but we've already got too much blood, sweat and tears in this little piece of dirt, not to mention a lot of expensive fertilizer. And to tell you the truth, the thought of you and mom in a hot tub... "

"Tell ya what: I'll have my Mexican hands truck-in and spread around on Great Grandpa's quarter-section as much or more natural fertilizer as you could ever hope for, at no charge to you except for minimal costs of shipping and handling. My steers may not produce much beef, but they're incredible, absolutely huuuge producers of prime... "

"We don't want any of your bullshit, old man," said the boy in a firm tone of voice. "It's full of artificial 'nutrients'—unnatural as tits on a boar, as you might put it—not fit for growing vegetables and grapes. That's final."

As Merlene's no-account boy turned his back and walked away from the sweetheart deal... "Okay, okay, think about it and get back to me," Jonathan shouted. He wasn't about to give up. According to his favorite verse from the Bible—a very special book of his, and personally autographed by a Pope who happened to be a close friend—there was more than one way to skin a cat, or squash a grape. Nevertheless, getting into the SUV, he was grumpier than an old maid on Valentine's Day, and even grumpier back at the Bunkhouse Motel, getting into the elevator that would take him to the second-floor penthouse he called home sweet home. Awhile later, stripped down to his longjohns and reclined in an aluminum trough filled with steamy hot water laced with *Cinnamon Buns* bubble bath—a Mason jar of buttermilk in one hand, TV remote gadget in the other—Jonathan further sought to soothe his chronic and increasingly severe case of red-ass, by clicking on a TV mounted to a wall across from him. Bill O'Reilly's big head appeared on the screen.

"Caution! You are about to enter the no spin zone. On tonight's Factor: Disturbing new reports that Hillary Clinton herself, not her closest aide's husband, disgraced former Congressman, Anthony Weiner, may have exposed her genitalia online under the alias, Carlos Danger. More on this troubling development from our panel of experts after this."

Jonathan looked at Fox News religiously, not because he had any particular rooting interest in political shenanigans—and sure as hell not to hear that O'Reilly gas bag spout—but to see the network's semi-good looking blonde gals, always smiling, claw for face time. Some nights, the O'Reilly show was more entertaining, and arousing, than the acts put on in back rooms of high-class Tijuana gentlemen's clubs. And about once every other week or so on Hannity's otherwise boring one-mouth gabfest, he would get lucky. For infliction of amazing, incredibly orgasmic scratching, Jonathan's favorite was the long, lean cougar, but... Two lesser Fox News kitty cats appeared onscreen, clawing:

"...would explain what she was so desperate to erase from e-mails sent and received by her confidential assistant, Huma Abedin Weiner. If caught lying about not having a penis..."

"That would be a whopper, alright. Hillary's entire political standing is based solely on her claim of being a woman. Unless she can show..."

"...she's a woman, but equipped to be a President..."

"She's trying to have it both ways..."

"Her spokespeople deny it's Hillary's big whopper. They admit the hacked video snippet may show slightly over-sized female equipment, not hers, which is classified, but possibly that of..."

"She'll have to prove it in front of a congressional committee, classified or not. If she is a man, a/k/a Carlos Danger, secretly trolling gay Republican males, she could be susceptible to blackmail by Donald Trump..."

"...not to mention the ayatollahs, the Chinese, the Chamber of Commerce, and other alleged conspirators on the alleged right..."

Damnit, the camera switched to O'Reilly. "Now hold on, ladies," the sumbitch said, "let's be fair and balanced. Someone who should know, Hillary's longtime confidante, Lanny Davis, is in our Washington studio, sweating, but otherwise his usual calm, cool and collected lawyerly self. What say you, Lanny: Penis or clitoris? I'll give you the last word."

"Sorry to disappoint you, Bill, but in the new transgender age we live in, it doesn't matter what the hacked video shows. By making Hillary the victim of yet another mean-spirited, prurient attack, I'm afraid Fox News has shot itself in the foot already lodged in your mouth. This is just more old news, Bill, already litigated ad nauseum in the court of public opinion. What you should be wondering about is whether Jeb Bush has testicles big enough to sit in the Oval Office, and whether Donald Trump's penis…"

"We do. We do just that, Lanny. At Fox News, always far and balanced, we wonder all the time about Jeb's balls and The Donald's penis. I myself have investigated both…"

As the Fox News bloviater began to read fawning letters from other viewers and hawk his ghost-written books and personal logo stuff, Jonathan shut off audio, but continued watching the screen for another glimpse of the blondes. He had no use for Hillary Clinton, an old gal with more ass than a government mule. And had no regard for Trump, who bragged like a tin horn Texan with more hat than cattle. He himself would be great as President, Jonathan thought. He would be huge, incredible, absolutely unbelievable in the lopsided office, but would never stoop to the whore's game called American politics: putting his name out there; getting his face on TV; crawling on his belly along the cheesy bottom of…

Mr. O'Reilly's clothes provided by Hickey-Freeman… Limo and escort provided by Trump Casinos… Groceries by Food Bank of America… Shoe Shines by Gus.

SEVEN

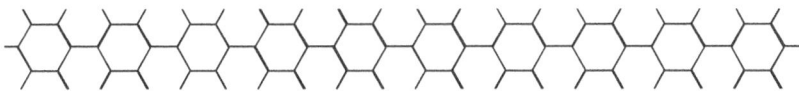

Hoping to find news to write about—anything not related to the subject of Gaylord Goodhart—Henryetta walked along Main Street. Maybe she would get lucky and see a man bite a dog or something. Maybe she would eye-witness a flasher expose hisself to… At the corner of 4th Street, there stood Mayor Buford P. Bailey, wearing a hat, dark glasses and a raincoat. Before she could ask him what in tarnation he was up to, a middle-aged gal with a big cardboard box in her arms got to him from the opposite direction. "Morning, Mayor," she said. "Are you not decided about expecting rain or shine? Today's weather report didn't warn about anything unseasonal, but you never know these days about anything."

"Shhhh!" he said, before looking up the street past the woman, then back at her. "Don't think of me as your Mayor," he said. "Think of me as an ordinary man… "

"Land sakes alive," said the woman, stopped in her tracks. "I thought all that talk about giving you your walking papers was just wishful thinking."

"It is just wishful thinking," he answered. "But talk to me like I was an ordinary man anyway, loitering on the street and… "

"I hear they're hiring at the Walmart," she said. "Have you ever worked a day in your life, say, as a check-out sacker?"

"Miz Haggard, please, just <u>think</u> of me as an ordinary man on the street, asking personal questions to ordinary women such as yourself. For instance, suppose a fine figure of a man stood right here in front of you, not wearing pants but instead... "

The ordinary woman took a step back from the unordinary-looking man on the street.

"... a wedding dress. Suppose he was a well known local hero, who..."

"I'm a married woman, and Charlie's got a gun."

"You wouldn't object, would you," the Mayor persisted, "if you looked up from the sidewalk and saw two personally autographed balls hanging above you? It's what the French call a three-part tableau and... "

Without looking up, the woman dropped the cardboard box onto the sidewalk and ran past Henryetta, who did look up but saw nothing out of the ordinary. "They are up yonder," the Mayor said to her, "at the 5th Street intersection. Maybe they need to be blown up to bigger sizes, for more dramatic effect."

The Mayor explained, "off the record for the time being," that the "tableau" was to also include two plaster statues: One that looked exactly like the old football player, Troy Aikman, was to go in the middle of 6th Street intersection, he said, pointing in that direction. And the other was to be put at 4th Street, only feet from where they stood. "It was made from a real-life mold," Mayor Bailey said, obviously proud as a prize hen layin' a blue-ribbon egg at the county fair. "They got Gaylord Goodhart to stand in a big tub of plaster from Paris, France, and... "

Henryetta like to have jumped back a step from the curb. The thought of passing by a statue of Gaylord everyday was hurtful to her, and kinda creepy.

"Well, I see there is no need for you to think of me as just an ordinary man on the street," said the Mayor. "I already know your public opinion, Henryetta. Obviously, you are just as bigoted as your boss, Harold Mixon, and jealous that it's not you who's going to be in that Ring of Honor ceremony wearing a long white dress!"

Henryetta felt blood boil up into her face. Before she could stop herself from lashing out at the truth of the matter, "What about you your own self, Mr. Mayor?" she shouted. "You're a lot older than me, and ain't married neither. Some people in town already wonder... " Ashamed of herself, Henryetta took a kinder angle. "Ain't there anything else for you to talk about 'cept Gaylord Goodhart?"

"Such as what?" he asked. "What else is going on in town that you care about?"

"Nothin'," she had to admit.

"C'mon, little Miss Know-It-All. What could I possibly say that would make you vote for me?"

"Nothin'," she answered truthfully.

"Well, there you have it," said the Mayor. "Times are hard for a politician to think of anything to make folks like him. Every dern thing is up in the air these days."

Despite herself, Henryetta looked up toward 5th Street.

"One ball is Troy Aikman's and one... "

Henryetta walked on past the Mayor, aiming to put a few personal touches to her background piece about Gaylord Goodhart for Mr. Harold, and write a big THE END to their silly little high school love story.

Back at the pink formica dinette table in her singles-only Shangri-La apartment, she re-read what she had wrote the day before, picked up a pencil and set out to tell the semi-truth from her unique personal perspective: *No, Gaylord Goodhart wasn't dumb*, she wrote. *He was just shy as a mail order bride about some things. Even after a certain high school cheerleader caught his eye — not one of the overly flirtatious big-breasted ones — he seemed totally baffled by her total lack of any defensive scheme. Her signals were plainly noticeable as a carbuncle on a nose, but by the end of the regular football season he hadn't even tried to score. After the Class 3A semi-final game in the state play-offs, they were sparkin' out by Possum Pond and...*

Henryetta put down her pencil, uncertain about how "personal" her reporting should be. Out by Possum Pond, she had took off her panties her own self and dropped 'em in Gaylord's lap. "Oh, I get the hint," he said, before blowing his nose, then handing the "hankie" back to her. "Sorry if I grossed you out, Henryetta," he said. Admittedly, it was dark in the back seat of her car, an old yellow Checker cab that she still drove. Maybe Gaylord <u>was</u> a little dumb, she had thought. The next Friday night, after the Henryetta Golden Knights beat the Little Axe Indians for the state championship, she took him home, and with the lights on in the living room, cut off his boxers with a pair of scissors she'd put on a table beside the divan for that very purpose. Wynona Sue was real proud, but...

... sparkin' out by Possum Pond and... Gaylord soon got the hang of things. He gave the certain cheerleader his state championship gold-plated ball and she started wearing his letter jacket, along with a semi-permanent hickey on her neck. That made it official they were going at it steady, and were one of the cute couples at Henryetta High. If not for the side effects of a school bus accident involving Gaylord's daddy, he and the only semi-flat chested cheerleader probably would have carried on like two rabbits in a gunny sack during their Senior year and got married after graduation, but... Henryetta left the next several paragraphs of her piece about like she had wrote them the day before, but then felt compelled to add a final thought from her unique personal perspective:

Gaylord Goodhart was still a fine young, red-blooded American boy when he left town, and by then his high school girlfriend had already got over him. Up until recently, she's had plenty of boyfriends since he gave her the mitten. Gaylord Goodhart was not the love of her life, and she wishes all the best for him and his teammate.

Henryetta put down her pencil onto the yellow paper, her head onto the cold pink formica dinette table, and bawled like a silly little ol' high school cheerleader.

WOMEN HAVE HAD THE POWER OF NAMING STOLEN FROM US.

Mary Daly, radical feminist philosopher

EIGHT

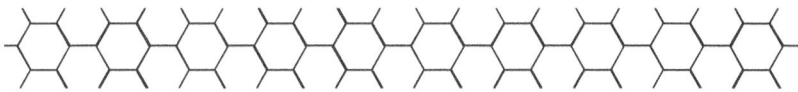

At the top of a hill on a dead-end street named Troy Aikman Drive—no doubt in recognition of some local politician who had done nothing other than mishandle public funds—Hilde arrived at the town high school, also new to her, but also worn and in obvious need of repair. Entering the gymnasium with Maude... To her chagrin, yes, instead of a chicken wire billboard, purple-and-gold banners along with a large sign proclaiming the gym to be **Home of the Golden Knights**. After printing her name on an adhesive label at a table where another copy of *The Squab/1965* lay open, she resisted an urge, barely, to again thumb to her Senior page and correct certain misleading information. An asterisk next to **Honor Society** and a footnote, ***For grades only***, were particularly annoying. She had not actually cheated in the Debate Club finals. She had only exaggerated, slightly, her Creek Indian connection, and only accidentally had misquoted something from a musty old article on file in the public library, titled *History of Our Town Up to...*

"Why, Hil-dee <u>Bottomly</u>," said a frightful, black-haired, overly thin, overly made-up woman, staring at her name tag. "Didn't you ever get married? Or are you divorced, and mad as a wet hen at your ex, ha, ha. You always were different, uh, I mean independent. Are you still, well, not a <u>young</u> Republican for Goldwater, but still picketing in favor of nuclear war with Russia?"

"Times change, Darlene," said Maude from beside her. "And some of us gracefully evolve. Hilde is the founder of the Homes Sweet Homes Foundation, based in Washington, and a proud liberal Democrat, like her husband, William Moon."

"Oh," said the woman, before scurrying toward a gaggle of other over-dressed women assembled under a wall-mounted scoreboard. "Darlene is still married, still to that nerd, What's-His-Name, the one with buck teeth voted 'Most Likely to Become a Serial Killer', by boring everyone to death. He's a dentist, and in fact some of his patients have died, in part from jawbone loss. Retired now, but goes to his office seven days a week to get away from Darlene, people say, and keep company with his stamp collection. She recently led a pro life demonstration on Main Street, demanding capital punishment for her aged mother, on suspicion of contributing to Planned Parenthood."

Circulating among members of her reunion class, Hilde was flattered that virtually all who had known her said she had not changed a bit. That was polite nonsense of course, but at the same time it was painfully clear that she—who looked at her own face in a mirror every day and knew herself best—had indeed only evolved in almost imperceptible increments. Everyone else—except Maude—had changed radically, suddenly it seemed, for the worse. In truth, she had always been of somewhat *zaftig* physical inclination. As for more important values, yes, she had founded a chapter of Young Republican Bombardiers for Goldwater and marched in favor of dropping atomic bombs on various labor union headquarters, but... For heaven's sake, Ronald Reagan was a rabble-rousing labor union Democrat before abandoning all personal principles and becoming a radical right-wing fanatic.

Republicans were so stingy with so-called taxpayer funds, even those borrowed from China. So yes, her values had broadened. She had gracefully evolved... "My, my, Hilde-lard Bottomly," said Cissy Golightly, smiling brightly with over-sized capped teeth wreathed in bright red withered lips, and almost as much hair on her chin as on her head. "You haven't changed a bit, still so... so sexy to some men: warm in winter, as they say, shady in summer. Tee hee."

"Why, Cissy Go-down-nightly," she replied, more brightly, "still so... so... 'feminine' and so... "

"Hey, Tubby, how they hangin'?" said a voice from behind her, that of a man who had rudely slapped her buttocks! She turned. "Oops, sorry," he said, red-faced. "From your... from behind... your hair... I thought you were Charlie Tubman, one of the hogs, uh, one of the football lineman in my graduating class. Sorry."

For crying out loud, did juvenile plump girl cracks still pass for wit in this overaged high school of a town? Losing courage to wage her previously planned counter-attack against such misogyny, "Let's blow this pop stand," she said to Maude.

"C'mon, girl, don't let them see you cringe," her friend replied. "The Jonathan is over there, holding court with his toadies. Let's grab some flowers from a table and take a bouquet to him; you know, as a peace offering to, uh, at least freshen if not clear the air. Ha, ha, ha... "

Instead, Hilde, her nerve restored by bitter-sweet memory, took a half-filled bag of popcorn from a table, wadded it into a ball, marched across the gym floor, and barged into the circle of males surrounding Jonathan Henry. "Hey, Stinky," she said, thrusting the brown paper "sack" at him. "Found this little package under the seat of a red Mustang in the parking lot, and figured you might still be looking for it."

The tall, still yellowish-haired reform school reject puckered his lips, tilted his head, and for a moment stared down at her with a look of confusion in his squinted eyes. "Oh yeah, I remember you," he finally said. "The whatta-pair... no, the whatta-<u>pear</u>-girl, spelled p-e-a-r. Still a perfect thirty - forty - fifty, I see, and still very, very stupid. C'mon, guys," he then said, tossing his head of fluffy hair toward an exit. "Let's blow this pop stand and chill out at my pad, where a chick's gotta be a perfect ten to get even a sniff of what's going down inside."

"You go, girl," said Maude," back at her side. "Now get your undies out of a bunch and make nice to our Mayor, Booster Bailey, for the sake of our Homes Sweet Homes project."

Hilde's friend and colleague led her toward a stage draped in purple-and-gold, at the side of which stood a portly, middle-aged, bald man, studiously looking at an index card in his hand and muttering. "Your Honor, I would like to introduce Ms. Hildegard Moon Bottomly, co-founder and senior official of our parent foundation, who has traveled all the way from Washington, D.C. for the privilege of talking to you about... "

"Madam, please, this is a celebration of our glorious past, not the time and place to dwell on dwellings for poor people." That said, His Honor bounded up a short flight of stairs to the stage, took hold of a mic and bellowed: "Welcome fellow Golden Knights and fellow Lady Knights. Welcome back to dear old Alma Mater."

As the bumbling small town politician went on to recount his personal, utterly unremarkable high school experiences, Hilde's nerve again wavered. Her ever-ingratiating husband was also a glib public speaker. People supposedly liked him, for no apparent reason other than his ability to "relate" to them. She, on the other hand, had been forever traumatized by the harsh exit interview conducted by a sexist high school debate coach fifty years ago, who said she was "shrill, insincere and disconnected" from both her rehearsed words and audience. Through the years since then, she had become even more self conscious when even her subordinates at HUD and the IRS refused to smile, much less laugh in response to her memorized lighthearted witty comments. So for her to cast a rehearsed pearl to this redneck crowd of...

"... let's join together in one loud voice," the elected asshole on the stage shouted, shrilly, "and yell, yell, yell for our Golden Knights to win, win, win... "

"We are not 'Knights'!" Hilde shouted, climbing the stairs to the platform. "But we are ladylike," Maude yelled from behind her. "Be nice, Hilde."

Hilde seized the mic. "We are Fighting Hens, and always will be," she proclaimed, to introduce her prepared manifesto. "As a woman, a once-proud honors graduate of this institution, and longtime resident of this community, I hereby demand that the proper name and graphic imagery of our mascot be restored, forthwith!"

The assembled old grads responded with hearty **Rah, Rah, Rahs**, which was exhilarating. Undeterred by an accompanying chorus of **Boo, Boo, Boos**, undoubtedly voiced by uninformed more recent graduates, she shoved the Mayor to the edge of the stage with her hip.

Rah, rah, rah, rah, rah, rah...

God! That felt good, like some people described sex, or in Hilde's case, like beating the shit out of Buddy for crawling into her bed, smelling of cheap perfume and sweet talking.

NINE

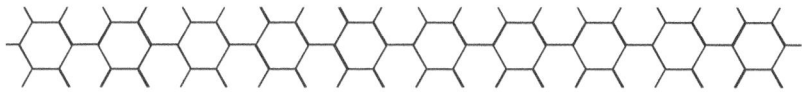

Change Golden Knights into Fighting Hens?!

Henryetta moved closer to the stage, where a chubby older gal in a blue pantsuit had took a microphone away from Mayor Bailey to make the jaw-dropper demand. "Back in 1969," she now said, "when I graduated from college in far-off Wellesley, Massachusetts, and began a lifetime evolution of becoming the person I am today, another distinguished woman wrote an article warning us of the Republican Party's ongoing cruel backlash against our hard-won advances in women's rights, that to this day amounts to nothing less than a War on Women!"

Boo, boo, boo, boo, booooo…

"Twenty years later," the out loud speaker shouted, "when I was on duty in Washington, after volunteering for public service in our far-off nation's capital, we lost a bloody battle in that war, right here on the home front."

Booooooooooooo…

"Yes, in 1989, a year that will live in infamy, a mob of pimply-faced juvenile vandals—proclaiming themselves to be 'Golden Knights'—desecrated the proud heritage of not only our beloved high school, but also the proud history of our beloved town, by trashing the Fighting Hens of Henryetta, Oklahoma! Now is the time for all good women to stand up and fight back!"

Boo! Boo! Boooo…
Fight! Fight! Fight…

Rah for the Fighting Hens!
Rah! Rah! Rah…
For dear old Henryetta, we will yell, yell, yell…
Boo, boo, boo…
When those Golden Knights all fall in line…
Rah, rah, rah…
We will fight, fight, fight for evermore…
Boo! Boo! Boooo…
Fight! Fight! Fight…

The Mayor stuck his big red face next to the chubby gal's big round face and hollered into the microphone: "Please, please, fellow… people. Please remain calm. This is a happy re-<u>union</u>! It is not the time and place to raise divisive issues between old Hens and middle-aged Knights."

Boo! Boo! Boooo…

"Take a stand, Booster!"

"Set on it, Thumbs!"

The Mayor stepped aside, looked right and left into the all-class reunion crowd, and shoved both his hands into pants pockets. The chubby gal raised her arms, and as the gym got semi-quiet, went back to talking like a het up Baptist preacher about her own self blazing a trail… "sparked by another courageous woman such as myself," she said. "Yes, a woman, another trail blazing woman named Etta Ray, who was the first pioneer to set foot in Pottawatomie County, where I later set down my own shoe. The footsteps I later followed from there to this humble hamlet were also those of the same Etta Ray. This town was called Furrs when she became its postmistress, but in 1901 its enlightened citizens recognized her noble public service by re-naming the town in <u>her</u> honor."

Rah.

Boo.

"For no good reason other than Etta's unfortunate marriage to a nondescript man named Beard, they stuck on his first name, Henry, which was a sacrilege typical of the era before women even had the right to vote. Well, though we have had setbacks in our struggle for gender justice, we've come a long way since then. It's time, it's way past time, for us to dump Henry Beard into the trash heap of history, along with other shameful relics of the past such as the Confederate flag and... and statues of Colonel Sanders."

Boo! Boo! Boo! Boo! Boo! Boooo...

"In the name of all local women, and our sisters everywhere, I demand that the name of this town be changed to honor Etta Ray exclusively!"

Change the name of the whole cotton-pickin' town?! To Henryetta her own self, the very idea of such a thing came as a shock. And no doubt that was also why the crowd got quiet as a patch of watermelons, then broke itself up into groups—all men in some, all gals in others; older old grads here, younger ones there—buzzing among their own selves while the chubby gal and the Mayor stood on the stage, glaring at each other like an old married couple at sixes-and-sevens with each other about who was gonna take out the garbage—or in this case, who was or was <u>not</u> gonna take poor old Henry Beard to the trash heap of history.

To get reactions, Henryetta joined a circle of elder men. "Don't see why it's such a proud heritage," one of them was saying. "The so-called Fighting Hens never won a state championship in football, not in my lifetime." Another said, "Maybe not, but except for that one year when we had Gaylord Goodhart on the team, the so-called Golden Knights have not won any gold balls neither. I don't give a damn what decal the boys put on their helmets, but by God, they'll unhonor ol' Henry What's-His-Name over my dead body!" About all the other old codgers mumbled "Amen" to that sentiment.

A nearby gaggle of mainly middle-aged gals was all in favor of going back to being Fighting Hens, but were even more het up, in a semi-personal way, about running Henry Beard out of town. "Etta Ray was the one holdin' down a job at the post office," one of them pointed out. "Her no-account husband was likely hangin' out at the feed store, just like my Roy, settin' by the cracker barrel, chewin' by the stove, and complainin' about the government, while their unattended younguns ran around like wild animals." All the other ladies also clucked disapproval of Henry. "And Etta Ray must have been a fine woman," said another gal, "for even the town men to honor her, when women couldn't even vote, for cryin' out loud!"

As Henryetta headed for a younger, mixed group... "Why, Hinryetta Heeburt," said a gal, who she semi-recognized as one of her own high school classmates. "Wolfie and me are livin' in Dallas now, and I guess you also heard about, you know, about Gaylord gettin' married to Billy Ray at halftime of the Redskins game. I never did know what he saw in you... I mean, you were cute in the face, but... Maybe it was your 'boyish' figure... and your boyish name." For the first time ever, Henryetta was not unhappy to be set upon by Mayor Bailey.

"Henryetta, for public safety, I hereby forbid the *Weekly Herald* to put out anything in writing about what that hysterical woman from Washington, D.C. said to rile folks up," the Mayor said, wiping sweat off his forehead with a rag. "The upcoming election is too important to get tangled up in divisive issues." When she asked the Mayor where he his own self stood on changing the name of the town, he took off for the boys locker room, maybe because he had an unpopular opinion on the matter. Or maybe because Maude Rouser and the chubby gal from Washington were headed their way.

"Henryetta, my dear," said the kindly seeming "Aunt Maude" from the local Homes Sweet Homes Association, who she had previously interviewed about putting up houses for poor folks. "I am so glad to see you here tonight," the old gray-haired lady in a house dress said. "May I introduce my dear friend, Hildegarde Moon Bottomly, who has something important to say." Ms. Bottomly—whose unmarried name must have been Moon—put out a pudgy hand to shake. "Why on earth would your mother name you 'Henrietta'?" she said in an unkindly way, "with an i instead of a y no doubt, but still... "

"Now, Hilde," said Aunt Maude, "lots of mamas in these parts put 'etta' or such onto the female namesakes of beloved brothers or uncles in their families. It doesn't necessarily do much harm. My little sister, Earlene is girlish as could be, except for unusually big feet and that dark mustache."

Maybe because there was somethin' unlikable about Aunt Maude's friend from out of town, Henryetta told Ms. Bottomly she had run out of paper in her notebook. "Not that it matters," she added. "My boss at the *Weekly Herald* likely won't print any 'news' about what you had to say here tonight, on account of our Mayor's worries about stirring up a riot or somethin'."

"That is exactly what Hilde wants to address for the record," said Aunt Maude, turning to her friend. "She cares deeply about women's issues and personally empathizes with the unfair treatment of Etta Ray Beard as a second-class citizen, but also cares passionately about her mission as founder of the Homes Sweet Homes Foundation. In no way did she mean to imply that our Mayor is part of any 'War on Women'. Isn't that right, Hilde."

"He's a man, and a Republican," Ms. Bottomly stated for the record, "but yeah, he doesn't look like the type who would personally fight for anything against anyone." And then, "How odd it must be for you to bear the name 'Henrietta' and live in this town," she said. "Wouldn't you feel better if you went by the name 'Etta'?"

Actually, about a year or so ago, Henryetta had tried to do that very thing, but most people who knew her couldn't seem to get a grip on calling her "Etta," and she her own self never got the hang of answering to it. But now, times seemed to be changing. Maybe she her own self should get in step with flux, she reckoned, and try again to dump part of her own name into a trash can.

TEN

With a window shade pulled down and *Out to Lunch* sign posted on the front door of his insurance agency's storefront office, Buford, up early on a Saturday, set about discharge of his Mayoral duties with a new sense of urgency. At the high school reunion fiasco last night, he'd been caught off guard by the shrill diatribe delivered by that female war mongerer from Washington, D.C. No doubt he would also be double-crossed by that pesky little newspaper reporter, Henryetta. Thanks to her and the next edition of the *Weekly Herald*, people were sure to find out that the foreign female agitator wanted to change the name of about everything in sight. So he was determined to calmly work out the political calculus of a position on the issues the trouble-maker had raised, before someone got the idea of changing the name of the Mayor!

Hmmm. About half the town's residents were women—many had cheered the female carpetbagger's speech about how unfairly they had been treated by Republicans, like him—but by Buford's calculation, the other half of the electorate were mostly men, and lots of them had loudly booed the demands for so-called gender justice hollered by Aunt Maude's strange political bedfellow. Even if he'd had time to float a dozen trial balloons in the high school gym, results would have been mixed, and contentious. Even with two wetted fingers in the air, gusts of public opinion blowing in opposite directions would have left him confused and uncertain about where to stand and what to say. As Buford tried to dope out a firmly compromised position that wouldn't offend anyone, the phone on his desk rang.

"Good morning, Mayor," said a man's voice through the phone. "*New York Times* calling. Lucky to catch you at work on a weekend, like me." Buford momentarily lost control of a minor sphincter muscle. "Leading into coverage of next year's Presidential election, we're taking a look back to the last contest, in which residents of your town—notably including you yourself—played such a pivotal role. What... ? "

"The coin was already sweaty when someone handed it to me," Buford blurted. "Sun was in my eyes... Someone sneezed just as I was about to... I was holding a microphone in my right hand and had to flip the slippery silver dollar with my left thumb. I got it right the second time, with my right-handed one."

"Yeah, I well remember your coin-flips."

"The *Times* said I had a thumb up my a-s-s... and that I was like a butcher who put a tainted thumb on the electoral scales to tip the election."

"That came out wrong," the *Times* reporter admitted. "We should have made it clear which thumb you used in successfully carrying out your assigned tie-breaking duty. My mistake."

Buford thanked the reporter in advance for correcting his error in the upcoming *Times* article, and asked if he had anything else on his mind.

"Yeah, well, I suppose that'll have to do as a retrospective angle," he said, "but while I have you on the phone: What issues are currently in play down there? What has people interested? What do your constituents most care about this time?"

"Nothing," Buford answered. "I have no opposition and expect to win re-election by a landslide."

"Nothing at all, huh," said the reporter. "Well, I suppose the Town of Henryetta, Oklahoma has had its fifteen minutes of fame. The hand of history, having writ, has moved on to... Hey, what's the name of that feisty little strawberry-blonde reporter down there? Loretta?... Marietta?"

Dang it! Here on a platter was a perfect, second-in-a-lifetime chance to launch himself into the national spotlight, and he wasn't ready. Hmm, Buford decided to steer clear of any possibly controversial mention of Gaylord Goodhart's statue, but... Hmm, he had to say something before *The New York Times* contacted Harold Mixon's biased "little strawberry-blonde reporter" for misinformation. Hmmm.

"Well, it's early in the process," he ventured to report. "Public opinion is up in the air. I myself have been too busy tending to other important matters, so I really haven't yet focused... "

"Okay, I'll call the local newspaper and . . "

"...on exactly which way the wind is blowing in what you might call the fog of what you might call a cultural civil war going on down here."

"Really? Culture war? That could be interesting. What issues have got heartland folk at each other's throats?"

Buford took a deep breath, closed his eyes tight, and took the plunge: "Some people in town, stirred up by an outsider, want to change the high school mascot from Golden Knights back to Fighting Hens, and even change the name of the whole dern town while they're at it. Others are strongly opposed. People on both sides are pretty het up, so I am trying to remain calm and... "

"Mayor, I gotta meet a thirty-day deadline. What is the name of that little strawberry... "

"... think about, just think about, a compromise that will

satisfy both sides: Something along the lines of, say, 'Fighting Knights' for the boys, 'Golden Lady Hens' for the girls; and for the town..."

Click.

Though frustrated not to have gotten a fully inflated trial balloon into the air in time to meet the hurried New York reporter's pressing schedule, Buford was extremely gratified that public confidence in his flipping ability would soon be fully restored by the world's newspaper of record and ... "Eureka!" It hit him like a blow to his forehead: Two thumbs, one pointed straight up and one pointed straight down... no, maybe one angled slightly left, the other right... would be a perfect, simple and direct design concept for his campaign signs! And like President Nixon, he could adopt a trademark hands-up/don't shoot pose—not with spread fingers to make V-for-Victory signs—with thumbs pointed in one direction or another to convey his convictions. Newly inspired, Buford decided to terminate his think-tank deliberations about war and peace with women and get back out into the air of fresh public opinion.

Minutes later, back to loitering, this time on the corner of 5th Street and Main, "Don't be alarmed, young man," he said to a longish-haired fellow who came within speaking distance. "Think of me as an ordinary man on the street doing a public opinion survey."

"Cool," the passerby answered. "I've got a lot of opinions about a lot of things."

"Such as? Taxes? Economic development? The name of... ? "

"Weed. Somewhere west of here they legalized it, along with homos getting married to each other. Some politician said that according to the bible book, a man who lays down with another man ought to get stoned. I'm straight, man, but I don't see why that should be held against me. And for another thing, I think this town... "

"Should or should not think about, just think about changing its name?"

As his constituent looked up, down and every which way, as if searching for an opinion, Buford began to question the intelligence of American voters. According to a *USA Today* poll, hardly anyone could name more than one Constitutional right or more than two of the Ten Commandments, while almost all youngish adults in particular could identify every single member of the TV Simpson family.

"Someone ought to get those footballs down from up there," said this particular uninformed youngish citizen. "That's my opinion."

Frustrated, Buford snatched off his hat and dark glasses. "I am not an ordinary man on the street, I am the Mayor, and would like to know if you have an opinion about the name of your own town?"

"Mayor Quimby? What happened to your hair?" came the answer. "Springfield, yeah, that's it," came the next one. "I guess it would be alright to change it, or keep it. That's my opinion."

After a few more heated but equally inconclusive encounters with passersby—at least some of which had recognized the name Buford P. Bailey and his undisguised face as those of their Mayor—Buford retreated to his insurance agency office, pulled down the window shade, and re-posted the *Out to Lunch* sign. Immediately, it hit him, right on the chin: He had ambushed his own self by talking to national news media, on the record, about the can of worms uncapped by that... that woman at the high school reunion. Now *The New York Times* was bound to make a big issue of a local skirmish in a so-called War on Women, about which he himself… Hmmm. Maybe, just maybe, the least contentious option for a new town name would be… Springfield.

ELEVEN

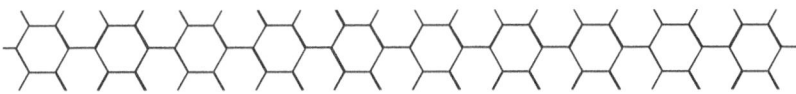

Henryetta stepped out of a shower and studied herself in a life-size mirror stuck onto the back of the bathroom door in her singles-only Shangri-La apartment. She looked about the same as always, she reckoned. Same strawberry-blonde hair, blue eyes, a few faint freckles on her face, and that dern front tooth: still slightly crooked. As for the rest of her... She knew better than to put stock in catty remarks made by gals about other gals, but still, the zinger zanged at her by one of her high school classmates at the big reunion—about her boyish name and figure being what Gaylord cottoned to back in high school—had stung. Admittedly, she had been a tomboy in her early years, but dang it, by the time she—and Gaylord—were Juniors in high school, she was not totally flat-chested! It was her name, double-dang it: Without even knowing that the town, and she her own self, had been named in half for a man—Henry Beard, spelled with a y —her notion that her mother, Wynona Sue, had put a curse on her was right as a trivet.

By the time Henryetta dried off and got her jeans, tee-shirt and sneakers put on for work, she was het up as a, well, as an unwet Fighting Hen.

On her way to the *Weekly Herald* office, she parked her old Checker cab of a car on Main Street, hustled past the famous "Doughboy" soldier statue on the corner, and went into the town's red brick library. "Howdy, Ms. Johnson," she said to the roly-poly librarian, who shushed her—even though no one else was there—then asked in a whisper what she was looking for, and pointed a finger to direct her to a shelf labeled *Local Interest*. Most of the books she saw lined up there seemed to be about rodeo matters—the town was semi-famous for hosting an annual "Living Legends Rodeo" on the south side of the Interstate, and had produced an all-time rodeo champion by the name of Mr. Jim Shoulders—but Henryetta had no interest in that particular local subject. She was looking for... There it was: On the spine of a checkered loose-leaf notebook, titled in handwrote letters, *History of Our Town Up to Now*. Inside the checkered plastic covers, she found what looked like a bunch of old high school essays, yellowed at the edges of their pages; some typed and some wrote with pencil on lined paper. She took the book to a table and commenced to read what a boy named Hughie Rice had typed back in 1957:

Our town of Henryetta, Oklahoma was once part of Indian Territory, and to this day is part of the Creek Indian Nation. It got started as part of a ranch settled in1885 by an Anglo-Creek man named Hugh (no relation) Henry, a member of the Alligator Clan, and a Confederate veteran, buffalo hunter and cowboy. But the town does not take even part of it's name from him. (More about that later.) He found coal in a creek (a stream of water, not an Indian) and started a forge for his smithy right about where the plate glass factory now sets. Railroads and mining followed, and the town that grew up by the tracks was called Furrs for some reason. (But that is not what there is more about later.) A woman named Etta Ray, the first pioneer woman to set foot over in Pottowatomie County, came to Furrs with her husband, Henry, and because she was the post madam, they named our town for them: Henry and Etta. (Which is what I said there would be more about down here.)

In the years that followed... Finding nothing more of any interest in the *C+* high school essay, Henryetta fired up the library computer. After about an hour of semi-fruitful research about names... Aha, she found that a famous lawman, Marshall McCluhan, was quoted as saying that "a person's name was a numbing blow from which he" — or she, no doubt — "never recovers." More het up than ever, Henryetta tore out of the library, hurried down Main Street on foot and barged into the *Weekly Herald* office. "What's in a name, Mr. Harold?" she practically shouted at her boss, who looked up from his scribbling with a startled look on his face. "Would a rose smell as good if it was called, say, a sweaty sock? I doubt it, which is why you have got to give up on that editorial you're writing about Gaylord's statue, and put somethin' powerful on the front page about correcting the name of our town!"

"What in tarnation?" Mr. Harold answered. "Henryetta, I can't be bothered with any such nonsense right now. This same-sex marriage issue has got me as stuck as B'rer Rabbit rasslin' with a tar baby."

Henryetta went on anyway, to tell what Ms. Bottomly had said at the all-class high school reunion about how the town had got named for an Etta and Henry Beard, and about what she her own self had learned at the library. "Ms. Bottomly went to high school here, and came all the way from Washington D.C. to demand that our mascot be changed back to Fighting Hens and the name of the town changed to... "

"Nonsense, people in Washington, D.C. don't know wet from windy, as a rule, and just want to stir up trouble. They ought to be worried about... about social decay in our country, but waste their time making fusses about... about the name of their own football team, the Redskins. I agree with the fella who said what they ought to do is take the name 'Washington' off the team for the sake of the players, who should be rightly offended to be associated in peoples' minds with no-account politicians."

"A high school in Oklahoma City got rid of its own Redskinned mascot just last year," Henryetta argued, "'cause it was disrespectful and hurtful to… "

"Bullroar," said her usually mild mannered boss, who she had never before known to use such a powerful barnyard term for nonsense. "Indian mascots honor native Americans' historical identity as brave fighters. They are meant to summon up warrior courage and ferocity in the hearts of their namesakes, and strike fear in the hearts of opposing teams. It's silly, but does no harm to either side in juvenile games of… When I played high school basketball, I never actually thought of myself as a 'chicken'. Players on other teams, and the cheerleaders too, called us 'peckers', but… "

That might explain a lot about men, and gals, of the older generation, Henryetta couldn't help thinking, before getting back to what was on her mind: "Our town—'Henryetta', spelled with a y—ain't like the town of Marietta over in Love County. Ours has a man's name stuck in front of a gal's name. And though most people might not know the reason, they sense somethin' queer about it. Believe me, Mr. Harold, I know what I'm talkin' about. I my own self have felt strange to be asked… I have had to explain over and over since the day I was born that my name… "

Henryetta took a deep breath. "Mr. Harold, I think it might be the two-sided name of this little ol' town, in particular as stuck onto me, that might have confused Gaylord in his formative year here, and pushed him toward same-sex gaiety."

To her surprise, Mr. Harold only put a hand under his chin,

like the picture of the famous statue, "The Thinker," that went above his **From Where I Sit** editorial columns. "That is just what I have been trying to say, Henryetta," he finally said. "It's misguided nurture, not nature that mixes up gender identities and sexual preferences these days." He lifted his head off his hand, set up straight and said: "The Missus has been on me to not write anything too powerful directly about Gaylord Goodhart, who is such a hero to our grandson. And not to spoil our little granddaughter's illusions about wedding dresses." Henryetta took another deep breath, as her boss seemed to inch along in her way of thinking. "Maybe I will be more subtle about the matter," he said, pushing his scribblings to the side of his desk, "and without expressly explaining all the reasons, come out in favor of changing the town name to… What should it be, back to Furrs?… Rose?"

"It don't matter," said Henryetta, whose grammar tended to wander when she was excited about something, "just as long as it's different, and don't draw too much attention to… to anything else goin' on in our little ol' town."

TWELVE

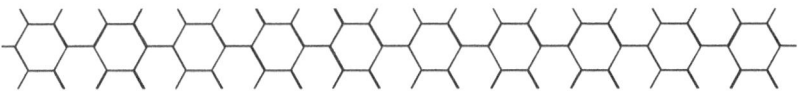

At his regular corner table inside the Chair Crushers Cafe—formerly known as the Pig Out Palace—through flyspecked windows Jonathan Henry could keep an eye on Kellogg's Korner across a road to the west, and another eye on Interstate 40, immediately to the south. Today he was less attentive than usual to the former—where Merlene's boy, Bart, was set on starting up an organic vegetable farm and vineyard—but was more than commonly interested in the cars and trucks speeding eastbound on the highway. From his motel business, he knew they numbered tens upon tens of thousands every day. And from watching Fox News, he knew they carried tens upon tens of thousands of illegal Mexicans. He had no use for that braggadocious New York fella—Trump —but he agreed with the sumbitch about one thing: There needed to be a wall put up on the border to keep those Mexican rapers from making it to New York City, where they could get their dirty hands on the Fox News blondes. Goddamnit, if he his own self was President—and by the way, everyone said he would be huge in the White House—he would protect the country's blonde women so fast it would make their heads spin.

"More coffee, Mr. Henry?" said the cafe's new proprietor from beside him. Though he had known Jorge for decades in different places, Jonathan watched warily as his host hoisted a barrel to his shoulder and re-filled a wash tub-sized crockery mug. "Made any travel plans for, say, Thanksgiving?" he asked the American-born Mexican. "Thinking of making a little getaway to, say, New York City, for the big parade?"

"Nossir, on that 'specially chair-crushing day, the whole family will have to work 'specially long and hard here at the cafe."

"Not interested in looking up a certain slinky little blonde thing in the Big Apple, huh?"

"Slinky thing in an apple? You mean... ?"

"Yeah, that's exactly who I mean, Jorge. You het up to hitch a ride up there to rape Miss Ann?"

Though not entirely convinced by Jorge's vehement denial of felonious intent to ravage Miss Ann Coulter, Jonathan returned to watching the eastbound traffic on Interstate 40, again grumbling to himself. The Fox News cougar, Miss Ann—blonde hair long and straight, black eyelashes also long and straight—had made a dazzling appearance last night on *Hannity,* to warn the public about the contents of her latest book, *Adios, America: The Left's Plan To Turn Our Country Into A Third World Hellhole.* Already it was a bestseller, though Jonathan himself saw no point to actually reading it or any of her books. Snippets, spoken by Miss Ann on TV, more than sufficiently got her points across and, hot damn, he loved hearing her talk in that stuffy nasal drawl—the very essence of "snotty"—copied right out of an old eastern boarding school like one of his ex-wives had attended.

What he liked about her even more was that unlike all his ex-wives—who had big tits—Miss Ann was long and lean. And he'd recently read a newspaper column by a guy named Barry, reporting that scientists had confirmed what he himself had always known for a fact: The primary biological function of women's boobs was to make males stupid. Last night, Miss

Ann had gone on and on about how Latino males were sex-crazed by nature. "Why else would Congressman Weiner have felt that showing his weiner was not in and of itself enough to catch a girl's interest; and that he needed to further tout his sexual prowess online as 'Carlos' Danger?" she asked. "Well, males named Carlos and Pedro and the like, they are dangerous, though to read or hear about about any alleged rape in the media, one would think only white frat boys ever committed the dirty deed. Donald Trump asked for an advance copy of my book, and read it cover to cover."

Damnit, all this talk about Donald Trump had started ruining the mood of Jonathan's nightly baths. Incredibly, Miss Ann seemed to have a girlish crush on the sumbitch. Hell, what could Trump boast about that he didn't possess more of? Though people said "The Donald" had a big mouth, Jonathan had noticed that actually the braggart had a tiny, baby bird-like oral orifice, with lips always puckered in a sucking expression. Even O'Reilly made him look small by comparison during interviews, and O'Reilly, well, he knew Bill personally. They had met in a hotel sauna one time, and like they said: Big mouth, small dick. Hmmm, could the opposite also be true in the case of Trump? Last night, the long lean cougar—flirtatiously batting her long black lashes—said Trump was the only one speaking clearly and logically, and: "I love the idea of 'The Great Wall of Trump'."

Bullroar!

Fed up with seeing how Donald Trump made Miss Ann's tail wag, Jonathan dialed 911 on his cell phone and went outside. Minutes later, one of the town's police cars—lights flashing, siren blaring—skidded to a stop in the Chair Crushers Cafe parking lot. Chief Potter got out of the black-and-white, and put a hand on his holstered gun. Jonathan stepped into his face.

"You're late, Potter," he said. "There's been a crime wave going through town for at least a year; you haven't lifted a finger to stop it; and by the way, my taxes pay your salary. Follow me."

With the police chief in tow, Tonto drove Jonathan across an overpass and onto the shoulder of the eastbound Interstate, where the two-vehicle caravan came to a halt. Standing beside the highway along with Chief Potter, he immediately pointed at a dilapidated van that drove by and said, "Look at that old junker and tell me what you see."

"Nothin' much," the town's overpaid top cop admitted. "Just a working man on his way to unstop a toilet, by the look of the 'Russ-the-Plumber' sign on the side of the truck. He wasn't speeding, and anyway this highway is... "

"Plumber, my ass! Damnit, this road runs right through town. Local residents living on both sides of it — helpless blonde women and children — they don't give a damn about stopped up toilets. They are too scared to go to the can or sleep at night on account of Mexican rapers... "

"I've had no reports of... "

"... comin' and goin' like Texas Aggies through a whore house on nickel night, damnit!"

"Well, there's nothin' I can do about Mexicans or Texas college boys unless and until one of 'em... "

"Put up a fence, right here in the geographical middle of our legal city limits. Turn the rapers around and send 'em back to the Rio Grande before they... "

"A fence? This is an interstate highway, Mr. Henry. The Town of Henryetta can't... "

"Bullroar! I want the alien influx stopped up. And until the fence gets built, I want you to park one patrol car right here, and another at the town's other ramps to the east, at the Indian

Nation Turnpike intersection. One of you can spot the Mexicans comin' through and radio a deputy up ahead to pull 'em over before they… "

"If I stopped any illegals on the highway, I'd likely have to detain some them 'til State troopers or the Feds took 'em off our hands. Our town jail will only hold five and… No sir, Mr. Henry; not without an official order from… "

"Don't worry about Thumbs Bailey; my taxes pay his salary too, and he's up for re-election," said Jonathan. "I might even let him put signs on a few of my properties at no charge, long as he doesn't put his name on them. Damnit, Potter, we've gotta do whatever it takes to stop dangerous Mexican rapers from having their way with Miss Ann!"

THIRTEEN

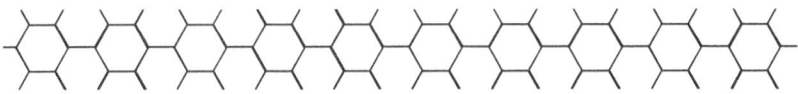

Coming into the *Weekly Herald* office just as Mr. Harold was coming out, Henryetta knocked her hurried boss off stride. "Gotta get home and help the Missus blow up a paper sack she's put her head into," he said. "Trying to fix those dern hiccups has got her out of breath. But I left a powerful editorial for changing the town name on your desk for you to type up." Then, over his shoulder as he turned away: "And oh yeah, Henryetta, you got a personal call from a fella named Bortz." Henryetta felt a little heart flutter. Back a few years ago, down in College Station, Texas—where she'd drove her Checker cab, hoping to prove Gaylord did not really kill his daddy and needed to be let out of the state penitentiary—she had met Benjamin Bortz, a young reporter who covered sports for *The New York Times*, no less. He was a sight better than ordinary to look at—dark curly hair, bright out of the eyes, lots of white teeth—and friendly toward her, only a red dirt girl from a little ol' town in Oklahoma. They had got to talking, maybe flirting some, which led to a semi-date for supper. And the next day he hitched a ride with her in a caravan that followed the prison van that took Gaylord back across the Red River into Oklahoma.

Henryetta found Benjamin Bortz's number, wrote on a pink slip Mr. Harold had put on her desk, along with his **From Where I Sit** editorial about changing the town name, also handwrote with a pencil.

Benjamin Bortz was only about twenty-five back then, but had already graduated from Princeton University and got a job at the biggest big city newspaper of them all. During the drive from Texas to the court house in Tishomingo, he told her he'd read what she'd sent to *The New York Times* about Gaylord's predicament—none of which had got put in the paper—and said he was jealous, 'cause her reporting had captured something called the *zeitgeist* of the final days of bigtime college football. He said that if it was up to him—well, it was mostly just friendly bullroar, of course—she would get one of those Pulitzer Prizes for her Gaylord stories. She'd had a little inkling he might be inclined to be semi-sweet on her, maybe even really a little jealous about her feelings for Gaylord, but then he went back to New York. Since then all she'd heard from him was that he was traveling around the world, writing about soccer.

So she was surprised by his call, and felt another little heart flutter when she picked up the phone, punched in his number, and heard his smiling voice come from somewhere. After they howdied back and forth, "One of the guys I work with was asking about you the other day," he said. "He's working on a retrospective piece, looking back at the last Presidential election and trying to get some background about that interesting 'little ol' hometown' of yours." He chuckled. "According to your Mayor, there's a 'culture war' going on down there that mirrors a big national issue about... "

"Culture war? Oh well, you can't put stock in anything Mayor Booster says."

"Oh," he said, sounding some disappointed. "The national so-called 'War on Women' is still news, but... Anyway, I guess you noticed your boyfriend, Mr. Goodhart, is on the front page. I'm covering the story from my Sports desk, and thought I might... "

"Mr. Goodhart ain't my boyfriend, not no more."

"… swing through his hometown, help my buddy with the local War on Women angle, while… "

"Oh," said Henryetta, catching his drift. "You mean that culture war. Yep, a feminist woman—Ms. Bottomly, who works with Aunt Maude Rouser at the Homes Sweet Homes Association down here—has caused a ruckus about changing the town name. My boss, Harold Mixon—who also went to Princeton, by the way—has wrote a powerful editorial on the war."

"No kidding. And what about local reaction to… to Gaylord's announcement, which also touches on a current national issue? What do the hometown folks—and your boss—think about their hero, you know, getting married to a teammate? Maybe I could kill two birds, as they say, by making a visit and… "

Dern! While she her own self had been trying to put a damper on that particular local angle… "Oh yeah, there's another culture war goin' on in town about that too," she said. "The Mayor wants to put up a statue of Gaylord, but Mr. Harold, and probably some others, are up in arms. Almost everybody must be talking about it, if asked."

"That must be hard for you, Henryetta, but… Anyway, I would like to see you. I'll do some checking around, talk to my boss and see if he thinks there's a hometown angle worth writing about. Why don't you send some ammo to me, maybe we'll cover these 'culture wars' on the front lines together."

After Benjamin Bortz ended the call, Henryetta got up from her desk, stomped a foot, and commenced to pace, while watching a wall clock like a gal in a hurry to get somewhere, waiting on a bus. By the time Mr. Harold bobbed through the front door, she was in a state. Before he could get to his chair,

"Mr. Harold," she practically shouted, "the more I think about the matter, it's noticeable as two pigs in a parlor that we got two culture wars goin' on in town. You need to put out two powerful front page editorials from where you set, and hurry up about it. One on the fuss people are making about that dern statue of Gaylord, and the other this one you already wrote on the fuss they're making about the town name, which I have already fixed to make it not so subtle."

"Well, I declare," Mr. Harold replied, settin' down with a look of puzzlement on his face. "People are already up in arms about mascots and the town name, that's for sure, but other than the two of us, and the Mayor, I haven't heard of anyone in town giving much of a hoot about the 'statue' subject. Nobody except you and I have even read my powerful piece subtly tying one issue to he other."

"But that's what your powerful comments from where you set are supposed to do: stir people up," Henryetta argued, almost directly quoting her boss from his past defenses of his inclination to write editorials. "Now pull up your socks and get that one about Gaylord's statue done in time for this week's edition."

"Hit 'em on the front page with both barrels, you say?" said Mr. Harold. "Hmm, I don't know, Henryetta, that might be too powerful. I might accidentally cause serious local hostilities to break out. Outsiders might take notice of us, like we are a bunch of rednecks. You know, Fox News, and the others too, they all the time seize on local stories and blow them up with sound and fury signifying nothing except what fits their agendas. But..." Her boss got that "From Where I Sit" look in his eyes. "In the approximate words of Henry V: In peace there's nothing so becomes a newspaper man as modest stillness and tranquility, but when the blast of culture war blows in our ears... "

Henryetta like to have wet her pants at the sight of Mr. Harold reaching for a pencil. She like to have busted a blood vein when he began to write on a fresh sheet of paper. If any local hostilities got heated up, by golly, she was ready, willing and downright eager to be a wartime correspondent in the trenches alongside Benjamin Bortz of *The New York Times*.

Gioachino Rossini/ William Tell Overture

FOURTEEN

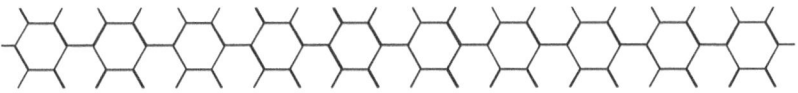

With bags packed and loaded into a rental car for her return to the Tulsa airport, Hilde again stood on the sidewalk in front of her childhood home, with mixed feelings. Despite extending her hometown stay by a few days, she had failed in her official mission to help Maude find a way to obtain the Mayor's approval of a Home Sweet Homes project. A minor setback. More importantly, at the high school reunion she had struck a mighty blow against the redneck town's sexist backlash against feminism, deserving of at least a Silver Star from NOW—the National Organization of Women—in the current retaliatory War on Men. Maude, who said she had caused quite a buzz with her demand that the town name and mascot be corrected, would now have to carry the torch single-handedly. Her own work on this godforsaken frontier was done, Hilde was thinking, when her cell phone ring-tone began to play *rump-titty-rump-titty-rump-rump-rump*... It was Maude calling, no doubt to again beg her to stay on the local war front a few more days.

"Hilde, thank Goddess, I caught you before you turned off your cell phone," her friend and colleague said, breathless. "A reporter for *The New York Times* wants to talk to <u>you</u>! Somehow he tracked you down and called me at the office. Hilde, *The New York* <u>freaking</u> *Times*, no less! They're following up on a local angle to a big story. Do you realize what this could mean for my project, and for the foundation? He's going to call you in five minutes for background, and quotes from the horse's mouth. I'll come over as soon as I can."

What a well deserved break! Probably the *Times* had tried and failed to reach Buddy in Washington. Fortunately, for Hilde, her nominal spouse and business partner was obviously out of touch, probably tom-catting in some exotic place utterly devoid of low income people in need of roofs over their heads — or rich people with guilty consciences — leaving it to her to hold the fort at this critical time. The Homes Sweet Homes Foundation was in dire need of a fresh face, so to speak. So was she, to be frank. And now that she was retired from government service, Hilde saw no need to continue discretely sneaking around in shadows to hide her affiliation with the worthy HSH cause. Excited as a gay young debutante about her coming out, she retrieved her briefcase from the rental car, hurried back inside her girlhood home, plopped herself into a living room chair and opened a laptop computer.

In the HSH project file, however, nothing struck her as remotely newsworthy. There was nothing quotable for anyone to say about simple facts and figures to a *New York Times* reporter. Comprised of forty residential units in twin two-story boxes, with outdoor grille and a see-saw in between, Hogback Manor was to be like countless other such developments scattered across the country. Its cost and required government subsidies were in line with standard... Hilde looked up from the computer screen. A deep crease crossed her brow. *The New York Times* didn't publish good news about good people doing good deeds. Was the reporter who'd tracked her down in Oklahoma a hit man, intent on "making his bones" as a so-called investigative journalist? Was he making an end run around her Washington lawyer, based on information leaked by someone on that silly congressional committee? He might have been tipped off by, say, the Happy Homes for the Hapless Foundation. Non-profit work was a cutthroat racket.

Hilde scrolled to the fine print at the bottom of the Hogback Manor financial program. HSH fees were in line, but if the *Times* dug deep enough into "Overhead and Miscellaneous Expenses"... *rump-titty-rump-titty-rump-rump-rump/rump-titty-rump-titty-rump-rump-rump-/rump-titty-rump-titty-rump-rump-rump...*

Hilde took the call, identifying herself as Ms. Rouser's assistant. "Benjamin Bortz, *New York Times*," said a man's voice. "As I assume your boss told you, we're doing a retrospective piece on the Presidential election of four years ago, when your County Commissioner contest became kind of proxy for the national race, and one of the local candidates, Virgil Carter, got picked to run for VP on the Democratic Party ticket. Now another of your hometown heroes is back in the spotlight and... I cover Sports, but volunteered to lend a hand with the local angle of our political story. Lot of unusual and interesting figures down there to report on, and according to a colleague at the Henryetta *Weekly Herald*, you, Ms. Bottomly, are now at the center of..."

"Figures?" Hilde was wary. Was she to be grilled about expenses of staff hair-dos and technical definitions of the term "overhead"?

"I take full responsibility for the many successes of HSH, since my retirement from government" she said, "but Maude is totally to blame for any unusual local figures. And my husband oversees foundation finances in Washington. Any suggestion that we were in the slightest bit 'cozy' with one another during my forty years of public service is completely groundless."

"Right," said the crafty reporter, in a vague tone of voice. "But as for politics, Ms. Bottomly, I understand that you—somewhat like Virgil Carter four years ago—have got the local electorate stirred up. Are you running for County Commissioner too? Do you think your message might also capture national interest? And lead to a shot at higher office?"

Message? National attention? Higher office?

"Perhaps," Hilde answered, in a craftily vague manner of her own. "For now, I am only listening, carefully. Exactly what message, that I may or may not have conveyed, have you come across?"

"I'm talking about your stand against misogynistic backlash," he said, "you know, in the Republican Party's ongoing 'War on Women'. Do you think that old Democratic Party slogan still has legs?"

"Oh, that message," she said. "Yes, I feel deeply about justice for Etta Ray, and will fight, fight, fight for Fighting Hens across our country if called upon for national service. You know, I first discovered a kindred victim in Etta when I was a girl back in high school, researching an honors Senior paper about the history of our beloved town. Etta was the first pioneer woman to set foot... "

Fifteen minutes later, after Hilde had delivered a somewhat expanded, more personal version of what she now thought of as her Class of 1965 Fiftieth Reunion Address, the *New York Times* reporter—following extended silence between them—said, "Wow, that's quite a load... of background. What is your view of the plan to erect a statue in honor of Gaylord Goodhart, there in his hometown?"

Aha, already, a gotcha question, Hilde thought. Who on earth was Gaylord Goodhart? A Confederate general? A County Commissioner? Head of some obscure foreign country?

Without responding, except by a coughing fit to simulate

static, Hilde shut off her phone, immediately re-opened her laptop and Googled *Hillary Clinton standing in polls*. Instantly, her own high hopes tumbled. Despite an off-the-chart unfavorability rating by the general electorate, Ms. Clinton continued to be Democrats' overwhelming choice for President. If nominated, she would be unlikely to pick another woman — especially a virtual doppleganger — to run with her. On the other hand, even *The New York Times* was yapping at Hillary's heels, and in the flux of the current political environment, anything might happen. At a *GoJoeGoPleaseJustGo* website she put her name, and Maude's, on a petition urging the sitting male Vice-President to get into the Presidential race. At another seemingly anti-Hillary site, she donated a hundred dollars from the HSH Miscellaneous Expense account to *MonicaLewinskyNude*.

Next, she started opposition research, and after fifteen minutes of digging for dirt... Maude rushed into the living room, carrying a loose bundle of placards that she immediately dropped onto the floor. "Got stuck in a meeting with our Mayor," she said, removing her gray wig. "He didn't say yes, but he didn't say no. So I made a contribution to his re-election campaign. Don't worry, nothing monetary," she added, looking down at the sheets of cardboard. "But enough about him. Hilde, what did the *New York Times* reporter want? And what did you tell him?"

"Get out of that dowdy 'Aunt Maudie' costume and take a load off your feet," said Hilde, rising from her chair and beginning to pace."It seems my Class of 1965 Fiftieth Reunion Address is resonating far beyond the confines of this small hamlet. The *Times* picked up the vibe, of course, and... " She wheeled around to face her friend and colleague. "Maude, I have decided to offer myself to high public office, and I want you to be my campaign manager!"

"High office?" said Maude, obviously surprised. "But… but… but," she stammered, "how high? <u>What</u> public office, Hilde?"

FIFTEEN

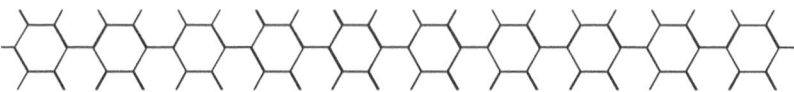

Ordinarily, Henryetta got haircuts at The Cutting Edge unisex salon over by the Walmart, even though her mother begged to do the occasional chore for nothing. It was worth paying not to set in Wynona Sue's beauty parlor chair— partly because the Hair House pet dog, Carl, was always humpin' her leg—but mostly because Wynona Sue, Ms. Pearl and Miss Crystal, who also worked there—and even ladies getting beauty treatments in other chairs— were always handing out free advice about how to fix her love life. But she had not been in an ordinary state of mind lately, and felt the need for an un-unisex setting to get at what ailed her. Having done her best to stir up things and lure Benjamin Bortz to town, she wanted to look her best in case he came; and if not her best, to at least look more, well, more feminine. So now she set in her mother's work chair at The Best Little Hair House in Town, looking at herself in a big mirror on the wall, and fretting. Wynona Sue hovered behind her, gently plucking at her hair.

"Most men like strawberry-blonde," her mother said, as she plucked, "and some men like about any color that's natural, so… You've got plenty of volume, Henryetta, lots of shine, but… "

"All men like big boobs," said Miss Crystal, the younger co-stylist, "natural or not. Ha, ha."

"…not much I can do to change you, honey, 'cept take some off and maybe iron-out the natural wave."

"Or put some on," said Ms. Pearl, "falsies, I mean. Ha, ha, ha."

"No, that won't do the trick," said Henryetta, in answer to her mother's suggestion about her hair. "Ain't there somethin' you could rub on it to make it get longer and maybe straighter, in a hurry."

"That's what they all say," Miss Crystal giggled. "Men, I mean. Ha, ha, ha… "

"Get him a little drunk and by the time he reaches in there he likely won't even notice the falsies trick," Ms. Pearl added. "Ha, ha, ha, ha… "

"No, honey, it's nature's way for hair to grow slow as a man gettin' around to poppin' the question."

"Get yourself one of those retro 'Farrah Fawcett Feathered Flip' wigs, Henryetta," Ms. Pearl suggested. "Men cotton to bed hair," Miss Crystal noted, "especially on gals in bed."

"…or, hmmm, I might have just the thing for you in the storage room, honey, a mess of strawberry-blonde extensions that Miz Harris' daughter brought back after wearin' 'em for only two or three hours, waiting at an altar for her groom to show up."

"I wouldn't have waited ten minutes…"

"Past midnight. Ha, ha, ha."

Extensions? To explain what "extensions" were, Wynona Sue put a magazine in Henryetta's lap and went to fetch the "slightly used merchandise." On the cover of *Weekly US*—headlined **THE GIRLS TURN ON CAITLYN**—a picture of a long-haired gal…

"I say 'she' is doin' it just to push Kris and Khourtney and Kim and Khloe, and even Kendall and Kylie out of the spotlight," said Miss Crystal about America's new celebrity—the husband

and daddy, trying to keep up with the Khardashian gals on TV—who recently came out and said that beneath it all, he too had always been a woman with a tale to tell.

"Yeah, I'll believe Caitlyn is a gal when she lifts her skirt and tends to that little thingy down there between her legs," Ms. Pearl agreed. Older ladies settin' in the co-stylists' chairs went to fannin' theirselves with their own magazines. "My, my, how times have changed," said one. "There is just too much flux these days to keep up with," said the other one. Carl, the pet dog, just laid there, not even looking up at her, Henryetta noticed.

Agitated by the turn in conversation, she had a notion to get up from the chair and walk out of the beauty parlor, looking unfeminine as ever, but her mother, Wynona Sue, came back with handsful of hair and practically pinned her down. "See here, honey, Caitlyn won the Olympics and got his picture on a box of breakfast cereal, but extensions can make even a real man like him look like an actual woman." Henryetta threw the magazine on the floor. "I don't need such an unnatural treatment as Caitlyn," she protested, but Wynona Sue handed her a different magazine and cooed: "You just set there, honey. Relax while I glue on one of two pieces of this one-percent real hair. It's a perfect color match, but if you don't like your new look when I'm done, well, I'll just cut it off to make you feminine some other way."

Only because she was semi-desperate, Henryetta tried to moderate herself, but immediately got more unmoderated after looking down at the magazine her mother had handed to her. "For cryin' out loud, why would you even have such readin' material as this in the beauty parlor?" The glossy publication was called *GENTLEMENS' TOPIX, For the Metrosexual Male.*

"We get a lot of such male types in the Hair House these

days." Ms. Pearl explained. "They set here like peacocks, admiring theirselves in the mirror."

"And the gals like to 'admire' the pictures of pretty boys in the magazines, don't they Miz Malone," Miss Crystal giggled into the ear of her customer, who also giggled. Henryetta her own self peeked inside the covers of *GENTLEMENS' TOPIX*. Sure enough, at the sight of a full-page picture of a man identified as *Metrosexual Icon, David Beckham in 2003*, she had an urge to lick it. As her mother went about gluing and weaving hair behind her, she began reading an article headlined ***Bending It Like Beckham: Long Live the Metrosexual Male***:

The great David Beckham, though now retired from professional sport, is of course the great British footballer who could kick a soccer ball so artfully it would bend around opponents trying to block his shots. For the completely uneducated, he was also the first celebrity recognized and rightfully celebrated for good grooming, taste in designer apparel and unabashed self love. Yes, the great Beckham openly shopped in the chicest boutiques, spent hours each day having his hair styled, his nails polished, his skin moisturized and—looking faaaabulous—being photographed. In short, he was the quintessential young metrosexual male.

But our unique species, dating back to at least the golden era of ancient Greece, has always been misunderstood by conventional minded people. For centuries we were consigned to the shadows of society, until bursting into the fashion advertising world in the Nineties. Even now, however, we are subject to a vicious ongoing backlash. Because we moisturize and enjoy aromatic candles, as well as herbal essences in our thrice daily baths, some people continue to say we metrosexual males are gay, and no doubt some of us are. But the vast majority of us who carry purses and embrace our feminine sides are straight as Jen Aniston's hair. Our sexuality and gender orientation are like oranges and apples, both fruity, yes, but otherwise almost entirely different.

Henryetta looked up from the magazine. In his high school days, Gaylord had never had any money for shopping, but had showed a certain flair for dressing up in one way or another. Sometimes he tied a bandana around his neck, and put different colored laces in his football shoes. He wore a silver ring made out of a quarter, Indian bracelets on both wrists, and carried stuff around in a little beaded sack. Gaylie was always unusually particular about his cleanliness and the way his hair looked. Was it possible the love of her life wasn't really gay? With a ray of new hope, Henryetta went back to reading:

...often accused by backlashers of being "narcissistic," like there was something wrong with what Sigmund Freud described as a man who loves himself, or what he once was, or what he would like to be. Duh. The original Narcissus was a good looking Greek youth who got tired of being hit on by his girlfriend, an air-headed nymph, Echo, who had nothing to say except to repeat what she heard. Boooring! He looked into a pool of water and saw that the reflection of his own more attractive image was a worthier love object than Little Miss Echo or anyone else. Perfectly natural that he would do that, and perfectly natural that he would later turn into a flower. Metrosexual males love flowers and floral-scented full-body after-shave lotions. But again, simply because we affect stereotypical homosexual ways does not necessarily mean we are all gay.

It is other males, naturally attracted to their metrosexual fellows and insecure about their own sexuality, who are the worst backlashers. Watching brutal sports or dumb game shows on TV in their non-designer undershorts, scratchng their hairy bellies, swigging factory beer—from cans—belching, farting, sweating and cussing, it is they—lo and behold—who never get laid. Except for drinking beer, Gaylord never did things like that, Henryetta recalled. Maybe he was just a metrosexual male, with put-on gay ways. *Now, alas, it's true; the great Beckham is getting old and perhaps a little unkempt around the edges. Some are saying that Bruce Jenner a/k/a Caitlyn, even older but now long-haired and pretty, is the new metrosexual man. Maybe so, time will tell how far "she" pushes the envelope. But memo to Caitlyn: Do not lop off that little thingy down there between your legs. Bend it like Beckham, but don't break it!*

"There!" said her mother from over Henryetta's shoulder. "How do you like the new feminine you?" Henryetta looked into the wall mirror across from her, hardly recognizing her new long-haired self. "Of course, just like Caitlyn, for you to get the full effect of feeling <u>completely</u> feminine, you'll need to apply some mascara, put a little shadow on your eyelids, a little color on your lips, get a frilly dress and… "

"Skimpy underwear too, or maybe none at all," said Miss Crystal.

"And either way," said Ms. Pearl, "to feel womanly and sexy, I recommend you get yourself fixed, you know, down there between your legs, in case… "

Henryetta straightened her back. "I don't need no fixin' down there!" she declared, pulling off the beauty parlor smock, then hotfooting toward the door. Wynona Sue yelled after her that a little "waxing along the edges" was all that was needed to finish off her re-do, but Henryetta—desperate as she was to be more feminine—was out of the mood to take anymore beauty parlor advice.

SIXTEEN

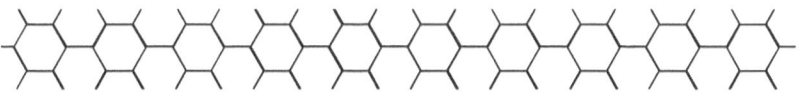

At a metal desk in the run-down Mayor's office—beneath wall-mounted pictures of former Mayors Bailey I and II—black ink poured from Buford's pen like bile from a ruptured kidney. His letter to the editor of the *Weekly Herald* such as an ordinary citizen named "John Doe" might write was in retaliation for a cheap mail-out, announcing that a <u>woman</u>—that dang Ms. Bottomly—was running for Mayor against him! *She's a carpet bag, not even a resident of our town until days ago,* he scrawled. *Though our duly elected Mayor is firmly opposed to Ms. Bottomly's plan to erect shacks on vacant local property, to show he has an open, totally blank mind, Mayor Bailey shook two closed fists at her sneaky accomplice, with no thumbs pointed in any direction, and gave her an armful of his campaign signs. This is the thanks he gets: a wooden stake in the heart.*

But if I know anything about Buford P. Bailey, and we all do know something, he will not rise to the bait, not lower himself to wallow in the mud with this porky pig from Washington, D.C. who thinks <u>she</u> --- simply by being a woman—is entitled to be the first of her kind to sit in the high seat Mr. Bailey <u>legally</u> inherited from his daddy and granddaddy. Our Mayor is always upright and will continue to run a positive campaign for re-election, focused on the issues that really matter to... Buford, almost out of ink anyway, laid pen aside and answered his buzzing phone.

"Bailey, get your big be-hind over here, pronto," said a voice that could have been none other than that of Mr. Jonathan Henry, the only rich man in town. Buford kicked off his loafers, pulled on a pair of hand-tooled cowboy boots, grabbed a small supply of campaign signs, and hurried from his office. Ordinarily "The Jonathan" did not directly involve himself in electoral politics; he allowed only his own name, not even those of his commercial tenants, to be displayed on his properties. But things had suddenly turned unordinary this time around. Flux was in the air. No doubt Mr. Henry, not only very wealthy but also a very, very smart businessman, was also outraged by the uninvited interloping of that... that woman. Being a Democrat, she was sure to be in favor of soaking the rich to pay for pot hole repairs. Her radical proposal to change not only the high school mascot, but also the name of the town, was extreme in the extreme, divisively divisive, and bad for local business. Being a "Hen," she was also bound to be weak on maintaining a strong high school athletic program.

Arriving at the Bunkhouse Motel, Buford was hopeful of getting Mr. Henry's support, but also nervous about what he would have to say and possibly even do in return. The bigtime real estate developer expected routine special treatment from various municipal agencies and officials, but aside from his proposed high-class nuclear waste facility— which Buford was now ready to wholeheartedly endorse—no new JAH Company project signs had been put up recently. In an elevator, however, Buford's hope began to cool. He broke into a sweat. Mr. Henry was known to be an outspoken private citizen, whose public pronouncements were overly direct and to the point. His references to women tended to be incorrect for politics, and his comments about politicians even more so.

The elevator doors opened and... Having never before been

invited up to the second-floor motel penthouse, Buford was awe-struck by what he beheld: A single large room, tastefully decorated with semi-realistic log-patterned wallpaper... Cowhide rugs, some with horned heads still attached, scattered on a raw wood-plank floor... For guest seating, saddles were strapped onto real log hitching rails... And in the center of it all, looking down upon him from barely beneath a low ceiling—the great man himself—astride a white horse whose legs had been cut off at the knees. In apparent reaction to his open-mouthed wonderment, "Easier for gettin' on and off her," his host explained, with a tender pat to the horse's neck. "And more cost efficient than raising the ceiling."Before Buford could think of anything to say, "Bailey, I've told that worthless police chief of yours to drop everything else and patrol the eastbound interstate 'til we can get a fence built," said his rich constituent. "In the meantime, to hold Mexican rapers for the Feds to pick up... "

Buford was shocked to hear that a private citizen, no matter how rich, had taken it upon himself to issue orders to Police Chief Potter, but then had to acknowledge that yes, of course, a taxpayer had a right to call the local police in event of a home invasion. No, he had not yet taken a position for or against Mexican rapers passing through town on their way to New York, he admitted, except to note that any and all problems on interstate highways were best left to the Feds. The town jail could comfortably accommodate only five detainees, he pointed out, and who could say how long the current administration in Washington would dally before taking illegal foreigners off the town's hands.

"Tell you what I'll do," said Jonathan Henry. "To keep those undocumented spics off the highway... "

"Spics? You can't say that word out loud," Buford protested.

"It might offend Spanish speaking voters, if we have any."

"Bullroar!" Mr. Henry bellowed. "'Spics' is just short for 'Hispanic', which is what they say they are. Same as 'Okies' is short for our kind. I've got a lot of Spanish talkers working for me in my motels, and they love me. I call the ones on my ranch wetbacks, and they think I'm just totally amazing."

"Wetbacks! My God, you can't call spics wetbacks!"

"Bullroar! It's what they are, for swimming across the Rio Grande at night. At least that's how they used to do it, 'til the damned Supreme Court gave 'em 'freedom to choose' other illegal options of rowin' and wadin' across. I say, make 'em get in line at the border, make 'em learn to speak English at a college level, know the law of the land, and fill out the proper papers."

"That's extreme," Buford argued. "Mexicans probably like to swim, just like us. They're… they're just wetback tourists without papers."

"Bullroar! Illegal aliens is what they are. No matter what those pinheaded college professors and you damned politicians say, I say call a spade a spade."

"Spade? You can't say that word and get elected."

"I'm not running for office, Bailey. But if I did, I would get elected so fast it would make peoples' heads spin. They tell me all the time: Jonathan, you would be a great President, you are incredible." The Jonathan got off the stuffed horse and fluffed his long yellowish hair. "Now, let's get down to business," he said. "To take care of any need for additional jail cells, I will donate this here Bunkhouse Motel to the town. How 'bout that?"

Donate the Bunkhouse! "Mr. Henry—may I call you The Jonathan?—on behalf of the town, I don't know how to thank you for your generous… "

"In return, all I want is for the town to give me a deed to that worthless Kellogg's Korner property on the west side of town, for relocation of my motel business, plus room for a casino and high-class drive-thru gentlemen's club for truckers."

"But... but... the town doesn't own Kellogg's Korner."

"Take it, by power of eminent domain for the public purpose of getting a bigger jailhouse. I've already had the dirt appraised, and will buy all the town bonds issued for the acquisition, at an almost fair rate of interest."

Buford, not very good at doing political calculus inside his head, scratched the outside of his head. Probably not more than a few additional cells would be needed for temporary detention of spics without papers, but the motel building could serve other public purposes. The penthouse, including decor, would be perfect for a new and improved Mayor's office. And almost as important, a new Bunkhouse Motel, casino and high-class truck stop would generate more than enough new tax revenue for the town to pay-off bonds for acquisition of Kellogg's Korner, as well costs of not more than about a hundred yards of picket fence. That kind of economic development, if announced immediately, would put a kibosh to that Bottomly woman's power grab and guarantee his re-election by a landslide. But, dang it, he would need to get various approvals from other government officials, which might be complicated and time consuming. If only...

"Tell you what I'll do," said The Jonathan. "To deal with the immediate emergency, demonstrate public need, and show my good faith while you're working out the details, I'll lease the entire Bunkhouse to the town — except for the penthouse — at a minimal *AARP* Shriners Convention rate, payable only as rooms are needed, plus expenses. Whatta you say to that, Mr. Mayor?"

Buford, though beside himself with excitement, tried to maintain a poker face. The Jonathan was reputed to be an artist when it came to horse trading. On the other hand, this was not his own first rodeo. "You'd have to sweeten the pot by, oh say, donating permission for some civic booster signs on your properties," Buford ventured to say, but... "at reasonable rates for your permission," he quickly added, after detecting the prospective donor's cool reaction to that particular counter-proposal.

"Okay, but no name on them," The Jonathan countered. "I don't allow politicians' names on my properties."

"No problemo, but... Seeing as how you're gonna get a new motel out of the deal," Buford said, surveying the room and trying to think, "to make it work for both sides, I will come out in favor of your nuclear waste project, but you'd have to throw in... the horse and saddle... or maybe just the saddle."

With the sweetheart deal done—minus the saddle and one of his own hand-tooled boots—Buford limped back to his current run-down office, picked up a fresh pen and carried on with his everyday citizen's duty: *Has anyone actually seen Ms. Bottomly papers? Does she speak Spanish? If she is a spic without papers and gets arrested along with other illegal Mexican tourists, where will she be held until picked up and taken to a federal pound? Our jailhouse is hopelessly undersized and outdated, as are other municipal facilities. The current Mayor's office, for instance, is not fit for human cohabitation. Unless Mayor Bailey is re-elected by a landslide...*

SEVENTEEN

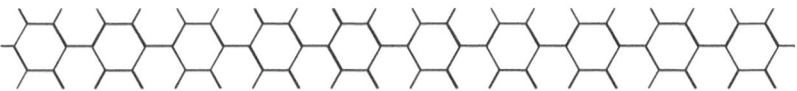

Though it was not yet eight o' clock, Henryetta found Mayor Bailey waiting at the front door of the *Weekly Herald*, huffing and puffing like a fat dog wanting to get out of noontime heat. As she unlocked the door, "Henryetta, you were at the high school gym for that danged reunion," he huffed. Following her into the storefront office, "You heard what that… that alien woman had to say about changing town history," he puffed. "Your own natural-born mama named you, her only begotten child, in honor of the town, for cryin' out loud. If that… that woman ever got elected Mayor and had her way, well, how would you like wake up some fine day and have people call you 'Etta'?"

Henryetta held her water. "Mr. Harold has took the Missus to a doctor in Okmulgee this morning," she said to the *Herald's* annoying visitor. "She's had a relapse of hiccups. So if you're het up to jabber with him about those dern balls in the air at 5th and Main, you'll have to come back later. I my own self have not got the time or inclination to wonder out loud about Gaylord Goodhart's fashion style, or choices of grooming products." Dang. The Mayor set hisself down in a chair next to her desk and took folded papers out of a chest pocket. "I've got new news for you, Henryetta," he said, unfolding one sheet and handing it to her. "This here certificate proves beyond a shadow of doubt I was born," he said, beaming at her, "right here in town!"

Henryetta glanced at the document. Only to jack with him:

"This here certificate is for a plain ol' 'Buford Bailey'," she said, handing it back to him. "It don't prove nothin' about …"

"I made up my own middle name later," said the man who somewhere along the way had took to referring to hisself as 'Buford P. Bailey'. "There's nothin' illegal about it. People change their names all the time. All you have to do to make it official is fill out and file a petition in County Court over in Okmulgee and pay about a hundred dollars, no matter how many letters you add or take off. It's as easy as changing your underwear or... By the way, Henryetta, if you don't mind me noticing: You oughta have your mama give you a haircut."

Though she had not wondered about the matter before, "What does the initial 'P' stand for?" Henryetta asked.

"Nothing, my middle name stands for nothing," His baldheaded Honor answered. "But that's not what you should be asking about, Henryetta. It's now up to the *Weekly Herald* to demand that… that… that … <u>woman</u> also prove she is qualified by birth to serve in high public office! And that she's a taxpayer, which I also doubt," he continued, while unfolding another sheet of paper, out of which a color photograph fell onto her desk. It showed one of his campaign signs: A red thumb pointed in one direction, a blue thumb pointed in another, and nothin' wrote on a yellow background except the word *Mayor* in black.

"Everybody in town knows the name, Buford P. Bailey, and I had no opposition when the signs got printed," Mayor (Blank) explained. "The thumbs say it all, and took up all the space. But now, because of that dang woman comin' into town, voters might get confused, which is why the *Herald* has a duty to put this here picture in the paper and tell citizens what it means."

Having already noticed some *Mayor* signs around town, Henryetta could see the need for explanation. One of them in particular, planted across from Kellogg's Korner on the road leading to the Interstate, looked like it might have been posted by a hitchhiker, undecided—or not caring—about getting a ride west toward Oklahoma City or east in the direction of Arkansas. And after seeing that the Mayor's second sheet of paper was a receipt for property tax on his Trudgeon Street bungalow, Henryetta reckoned Mayor "Thumbs" was right about something for once: It truly was her responsibility as a news reporter to look into Ms. Bottomly's local affairs. Her dream had always been to get a job at a big city newspaper and someday win one of those Pulitzer Prizes for good journalism. And though a local Mayoral election ordinarily wouldn't amount to much, with two culture wars going on in her little ol' hometown, who could say for sure what might happen in these times of flux?

Henryetta shooed Mayor Bailey off his perch and off the premises. Not knowing where Ms. Bottomly resided, she too then left the *Weekly Herald* office and walked along Main Street toward the nearby local headquarters of the Homes Sweet Homes Association. In the course of doing a piece about planned development on and around a hogback hill out west of downtown, she had previously interviewed the executive director of HSH, Ms. Maude Rouser a/k/a "Aunt Maude," who had wanted to squeeze affordable apartments in between high-class Spanish mansions that were to be built on the property soon as a golf tournament on TV drew attention to the possibilities. Like most plans for improvements in her little ol' hometown, however, the project had come to nothin'. And now Ms. Rouser was reported to be looking around for another place to put up "Hogback Manor." She had introduced Ms. Bottomly as founder of a Home Sweet Homes parent foundation in Washington, and a friend, so Henryetta reckoned the old gray-haired lady would likely know where to find the chubby gal who was running for Mayor.

As usual, the front door of the HSH Association office was locked and the window shade pulled down. Henryetta mashed a doorbell button, waited, then mashed it again. Someone inside pulled back an edge of the shade, and Ms. Rouser's wrinkled, homely face appeared on the other side of the glass. The door opened about halfway. "It's me, Aunt Maude, it's Henryetta, from the paper," she explained, "I just got my hair extended, that's all."

"Well, well, well, the paparazzi digging for dirt, I see," said the executive director of the do-good association, closing the door down to a crack. "Hilde has a listening engagement this morning out at the Rocking R&R rest and rehab ranch, and left strict instructions... But, oh well, I suppose it would be alright if I just leaked a few... " Henryetta had to semi-push the door open to get inside the office, which—furnished with a fluffy divan and rocking chair, decorated with flowery rugs and curtains—looked like a cozy old-fashioned parlor where old ladies would set and drink coffee. "Does Ms. Bottomly live here?" she asked. "I couldn't find no listed address for her and wondered... " Aunt Maude noticeably grimaced.

"Oh no, this is not the candidate's legal residence," said the HSH executive director, standing there in a floral house dress buttoned up to a lace collar around her ample neck—but with hands on her hips and her warty chin stuck out—looking more like some kind of security guard than anybody's kindly old aunt. "And we are _not_ using these tax exempt premises for political purposes!" she added.

Henryetta explained that she just wanted to ask Ms. Bottomly where in town she lived, how long she had been a local resident, whether she had any receipts for real estate taxes or rent, and if she was registered to vote for her own self in the upcoming election. Ms. Rouser commenced to grind her teeth.

"Oh my, you are a young whipper-snapper," she said, in a semi-friendly tone of voice, but with eyes squinted almost shut behind her rimless granny glasses, "by which I mean to say," she said, with a smile thin as an undertaker's, "only that you were not even born when Hilde was called to public service in our nation's capital and began to commute — like a Congresswoman would do — from her legal residence on Division Street to Washington, D.C. As for local voting by secret ballot, my goodness, child, given her positions at HUD and the IRS, that would have been a hidden conflict of interest. Hilde is an open book, honest to a fault, moral, ethical and uncorrupted as a cloistered Mother Superior. Unlike... "

Aunt Maude reached into a pocket of her house dress and brought out a hankie. "I really shouldn't leak this," she said, with her nose buried in the hankie, "but strictly off the record, well, just last week when I went to see Mayor Bailey about my Hogback Manor project, he raised two clinched fists, and by the look in his eye... " She put the hankie to her mouth and semi-whispered through it: "My mister used to look at me that way when he came home drunk from choir practice, so I knew it would be futile to resist. Fortunately a phone lying on the desk beside me interrupted his intended assault. Otherwise, well... But I don't want to stir up *ad hominem* rumors about Mayor Bailey. All men in positions of authority are like that toward strong women, which is why Hilde and I organized the Dicksy Chix when we were in high school: To fight, fight, fight...

"Here, let me show you — not as a paid political supporter, mind you, simply as a lifelong friend — who Hilde really is," said Aunt Maude, back to sounding kindly, as she grabbed Henryetta's arm and led her into a small dining room. A stack of thinnish books, that looked like identical copies of the same thing, set on a table next to a box of magic marker pens. Ms. Rouser opened one of the hardbound volumes, titled *The Squab/1965*, to a page containing a photo, semi-recognizable and officially identified in print as **HILDEGARD BOTTOMLY**, and below that, more informally as ***Little Beaver***. Henryetta also took note of the Mayoral candidate's record of high school achievements: ***National Honor Society###... Girls Bathroom Monitor... Dicksy Chix Barbershop Quartet... Fighting Hens #### Queen #################...*** *Debate Club* 1ST PLACE... PRESIDENT OF *Student Council #######...* ***Most Likely to ##########*** ELECTED PRESIDENT OF THE UNITED STATES... #

Aunt Maude sighed. "Student editors and poor old Mr. Quickie's Make-Ur-Own print shop and drivers license agency didn't have fancy computers and printers back in those days," she said, which Henryetta took to be an explanation of the mark-ups and handwrote corrections on Ms. Bottomly's high school yearbook page. "Has, uh, Ms. 'Little Beaver' come up with a design for campaign signs?" Henryetta asked, trying to sound informal and friendly. "Signs and slogans are pretty much what elections for Mayor amount to around here, and Mayor Booster's signs—everybody calls him, uh, 'Booster'—are, well, sorta confusing."

"Oh yes," said Ms. Rouser, with a big grin. "On a pure mauve background, in bright pink: simple, straight forward and... I happen to have a few of Hilde's signs right here," she said, stooping to take a quilt off a big pile of cardboard placards stacked in a corner. On what looked to Henryetta like a plain ol' light purple background, printed in bright pink: *I AM WOMAN!* was all it said.

"Yes, that says it all about why Hilde deserves to be our town's Commander and Chief Executive," Ms. Bottomly's lifelong friend said, holding the sign out from her to focus her granny glasses: 'I am woman, hear me roar!'"

EIGHTEEN

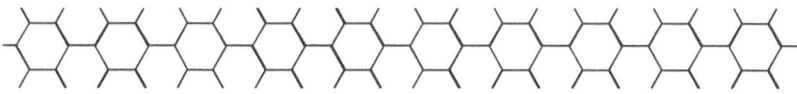

After a full day out at his JAH Ranch, watching a prize bull service a herd of cows, Jonathan returned to the JAH Bunkhouse, hungry and with an itch. Looking forward to a possible appearance by Miss Ann that evening, he immediately clicked on the bathroom TV, turned a spigot to fill the penthouse hot trough with steamy water, and stripped down to his longjohns. Sitting on the closed lid of the nearby stool, he waited for supper to be served…waited some more and…"What the hell?!" In the doorway stood that fat gal, What's-Her-Name, who had chaffed his cheeks at the high school reunion, and years ago had… Jonathan leapt to his feet. "How in hell did you get in? And what the hell do you want?"

"I told the downstairs staff you asked for this," she replied, holding out a covered dish with both hands. Jonathan stepped back from the bowl. "Fool me once, shame on you," he said. "Fool me twice…"

"I made it myself," she said, which was not necessarily reassuring. "It's a tuna casserole: My way of saying, let's put it all behind us and make a deal."

Because he was starving, Jonathan tentatively accepted the peace offering, sniffed it, and sat back down on the stool. The unpleasingly plump gal handed him a fork and announced she was running for Mayor. So what?

"Running to win," she added. "I'm here to do whatever it

takes to get you to back me instead of ..."

"You're out of luck," Jonathan said, after gulping down a mouthful of tuna casserole. "I don't have time for politics."

"Thumbs Bailey has signs on your properties."

"He's already Mayor. We made a deal."

"Get behind me. Together we can own this town and..."

"I already own this town," Jonathan answered, slurping a noodle.

"...use the Mayor's office..."

"I already have an incredible office."

"...as a stepping stone to higher office, and bigger deals."

"Like I said: I already have a high office, and I don't waste time on petty politics."

The chubby gal fluttered her eyelashes and stepped closer. "Virgil Carter, running for County Commissioner last time, almost got to within a heartbeat of the highest office in the land. Just imagine," she said, holding up her hands to frame an imaginary picture: 'JAH Bunkhouse Motel', in neon, on the White House lawn!"

Jonathan put the now empty bowl on the bathroom floor and listened to the So-and-So's proposition.

"Think what you could charge for a night in the Lincoln bedroom, even to *AARP*Shriners, who could roll in cots, bring their own sleeping bags, spend every dime they have on the mini-bar and pay-per-view movies. It could be huuuge!"

Jonathan had to admit to himself that he had got older—closer to "closing time," so to speak—and that even this zafty gal had started to look, well, not "prettier," but not downright coyote-ugly. "Why not get out of that pantsuit and into the hot trough with me," he said, rising from the stool. "We can watch the cable news shows and talk about..."

Hot damn, she was easy. Before he got around to asking what her name was, the chubby gal was down to her undies and up to her chin in hot water and *Cinnamon Buns* bubbles. "Call me Little Beaver," she said, "and I won't call you Stinky. I promise." She didn't look much like a little beaver, certainly not like a cougar—more like a hippo, relaxing in a bubbly wallow—but what the hell.

After trying to get in the trough with her, without success, Jonathan returned to sitting on the stool. He didn't want to miss out on a chance to see Miss Ann, but...Click. The TV picture changed, audio came on. A man's large head appeared on the screen. "Let's watch *Hardball* on MSNBC," Little Beaver said. "Chris Matthews is one of us, but you can always tell what he really thinks of Hillary."

The head, even bigger than O'Relly's, began to talk: "Earlier today," it said, "from somewhere in space, former NASA scientist, James Hansen, announced alarming new findings. The famous discoverer of variable weather—who in recent years has focused on progressive activism to save the world—now says changes in the political atmosphere of the United States, collectively known as flux, are a new imminent threat to human survival. Having stowed away on a space flight, intending only to correct those infernal satellite measurements of global temperatures, Dr. Hansen admits that he stumbled upon the new phenomenon that was completely unforeseen in his earlier computer models. To further explain, the noted atmospheric physicist himself speaks to us tonight from..." The TV talker, Mathews, looked upward. "Are you still in orbit, Dr. Hansen? Can you hear me?"

"Yes, still going 'round and 'round," said a male voice, "and since my latest spin, the evidence of flux has become even clearer. Sharply decreased levels of estrogen, not emissions of CO_2, are the root cause of all our problems. With feminine instinct now virtually <u>ex</u>tinct, American politics can no longer efficiently function in the Seinfeld model of being about nothing. The self sustainability of our current establishment is severely threatened by erosion of safe, albeit mushy middle grounds for our leaders to stand upon in swamps of seething testosterone belching dangerous vapors of unmitigated public anger."

"Aha," said Matthews, as spittle ran down his upturned chin. "So that is the scientific explanation for the popularity of that swaggering yellow-haired buffoon, Donald Trump, and the reason we're confronted by that African-American quack doctor, Carson."

"Yes, and also that unblonde Italian businesswoman—God bless her—who likewise has no political bona fides. Flux is out of control, and it's not funny."

Jonathan glanced at Little Beaver, staring at the TV screen with big blue eyes. Matthews returned to facing the camera. "From among the many experts who have hailed Dr. Hansen's startling breakthrough," he said, drooling, "joining us tonight by phone is *New York Times* political science editor, Candi Ochs Sulzberger. Tell us, Candi, what does it all mean?"

"In an article six years ago, our reporter expressly wished that Dr. Hansen would stick to what he really knows," said a high-pitched female voice. "Now, thankfully, the science is settled, the debate is over: There is way too much yang and nor half enough yin in the atmosphere. Hopefully, we can now find ways to reverse the imbalance, restore the natural effeminate political environment, and get back to business as usual. You know, without women's votes and injection of massive amounts of estrogen into the American political system, no Democrat would have won the Presidency since 1950, except Lyndon Johnson in the aberrational year of 1964, when even men were scared shitless that his Republican opponent, General Goldwater, would start a nuclear war with Russia."

The MSNBC host scowled, in anticipation, it seemed, of what Candi would likely say next. And sure enough, without naming names: "In other words, Chris, in this current time of emergency, it is critical to human survival that we finally elect a woman to be President of the United States!"

"Or a Beta male such as Al Gore," the *Hardball* guy sputtered. "Maybe even an openly transgender person such as Caitlyn Jenner, or now that Bill has been gelded..."

"Absolutely not!" shouted—not the voice of Candi Ochs Sulzberger—but the also shrill voice of Dr. Hansen. "America is at the tipping point of catastrophic national menopause. To survive, we need to get real women involved, young big-breasted blondes, and lots of them."

Jonathan again turned his attention to Little Beaver, who fluffed her blondish hair, coaxed a mass of bubles into her chest, and winked. "Hey, big spender," she said. "It's getting a little tepid in the trough. How about you cranking up your burner, and taking another shot at getting behind me."

Hot damn, just as one of Jonathan's favorite Bible verses said: Where there was enough of a will, there was always enough of a way, sometimes barely, to get a deal done.

NINETEEN

As always when crossing the Arkansas River in her yellow Checker, which was seldom, Henryetta's thoughts wandered back to when she thought she was on her way to winning one of those Pulitzer Prizes. Mr. Harold had bought a big city newspaper—she'd thought—and had hired her to come up to Tulsa to cover world affairs—she'd thought. Only when she got to her new desk did she realize that all there was to her so-called roving correspondent job was to take pictures and write captions about "world affairs" in the Tulsa suburb of Chelmsford Heights for Mr. Harold's new weekly paper called *Weekender World*. Now, where the Chelmsford Heights Mall used to be, a sign identified a big grassy field sprinkled with gravestones as a "memorial park." And across a road in the separate town of Fiddler's Green, on a parcel of land that had been a cemetery before the mall burned down, now there was an open-air shopping center called Mason-Dixon Promenade. A fancy women's clothes store in the so-called lifestyle center, Miss Margaret's of Fiddler's Green, would be just the place to find a frilly dress to make her look more feminine, Henryetta reckoned.

Not caring how much such a re-do would cost—fellas like Benjamin Bortz were rarer than good weather in Okmulgee County—she parked her Checker and went on in the store that was grandly decorated with Chinese rugs on a marble floor, a crystal chandelier hanging from a high ceiling and—to her surprise— now lots of dresses hung on racks. Miss Margaret's had never before been much like the Walmart, but... A figure in black appeared from somewhere like a trick-or-treater on Halloween. "Bless my soul," said the semi-youngish man, who had waited on her awhile back, when Mr. Harold was treating. "Could it possibly be our long gone roving correspondent, Miss Henryetta, spelled with a y?" A silver nameplate matching a silver earring reminded her he was an "Andy."

"My goodness," he said, "your hair—so ... so 'Caitlyn'—and almost one percent human. I didn't realize they grew strawberry-blonde locks in Mexico."

Before she could state her business, Henryetta glimpsed—of all people—Aunt Maude and Ms. Bottomly, outfitted alike, darting into a dressing room in the rear of Miss Margaret's. Andy must have caught her glance, and no doubt a look of surprise on her face. Aunt Maude was inclined to wear ordinary old-fashioned house dresses, but Henryetta's impression of Ms. Bottomly big city style was... "Oh yes," Andy said in a lowered voice, "this is what it has come to: so-called women engaged in so-called shopping for 'pantsuits'! I mean, really, Henryetta," he said, eyeing her own regular jeans-blouse-and-sneakers outfit, "someone such as yourself, young and, uh, naturally androgynous, can almost pull off a grungy Euro-trash look, but that 'person' wanting a pantsuit... "

Androgynous?

"What?" Andy sputtered. "Does that chubby one in the matching, equally deplorable so-called 'house dress' think this is a Sherwin-Williams paint store, stocked with triple-X Large-size overalls?"

Andy went on to complain that the "Caitlyn craze" had "wrought havoc" in Miss Margaret's business. "Yes, women's fashion is itself flux, flux itself is fashion, an irresistible force of nature that can obliterate so-called immovable mountains," he said, smoothing out an eyebrow with a pinky finger. "But when flux meets flux in everything around it: Chaos!" The semi-prissy dress salesman said that in backlash reaction to Caitlyn, "the new feminine is masculine."

Again he eyed her head to foot. "Women who used to be our best customers now come in here looking almost like you," he said, "wanting sweatpants, of all things! Some actually sweating, after jogging from home, trying to look 'fit', even muscular; desperately fearful someone will suspect them of being a *faux* female *a la* Caitlyn. How could we have foreseen such madness?" Henryetta noticed Andy's own forehead had started to glisten. "Yes, we are getting some metrosexual male foot traffic," he said, "but they're mostly just loungewear lookers, waiting to see how the flux flows. We can't give away our frilly frocks."

Even so, after peeking at a *50% OFF* price tag hanging out of the neck of a frilly frock, Henryetta reckoned she had better go shopping somewhere else. But then, when Andy scooted toward a possibly metrosexual male who wandered into the store, she reckoned she would first try to interview Ms. Bottomly, who so far had acted like she didn't have to actually campaign to be elected Mayor. At the rear of Miss Margaret's, Henryetta knocked on the door of the dressing room where the bashful candidate and her longtime friend... Aunt Maude came out, closed the door behind her and leaned back against it.

"Well, well, well, the paparazzi never rest, I see," the kindly old woman said, with an unkindly frown on her homely face. "Following a scent of scandal all the way to Fiddler's Green, are we? My dear, don't you have the decency to respect Hilde's few moments of privacy?"

Henryetta was took aback. She her own self was all in favor of Ms. Bottomly's demand for changing the town's name, and changing the town's Mayor too, but reckoned she shouldn't say so out loud. She explained to Aunt Maude that she wasn't following the Mayor candidate's odor of scandal, and only wanted to get a few quotes for an editorial being wrote by her boss, Mr. Harold.

"Hilde is in conference," Aunt Maude answered. "She is on the phone, consulting with a certain 'Very Important Person' in Washington. We will e-mail her own words to the media, all in good time." And with that, Ms. Bottomly's friend went back into the dressing room and slammed the door shut behind her. Henryetta turned to go, but...

"Well, well, well," said another figure in all black, "Miss Henryetta, a women's fashion trendsetter, as it turns out, except for the hair extensions." She was Andy's co-clerk, an "Amanda," Henryetta recalled, and—loaded down with an armful of dresses of different colors—seemed not so ready to give up on getting Ms. Bottomly out of pantsuits and into *faux* feminine "Caitlyn" style outfits. "This may take awhile, my dear," she said, "so you will have come back later. I mean, really, you must have noticed: Your friend has one blue eye and one brown, making it almost impossible to coordinate frocks for her, poor dear."

Henryetta decided she her own self would give up on "her friend" for the time being, and try to coordinate a frilly frock for her own self at a nearby J.C Penny's store.

TWENTY

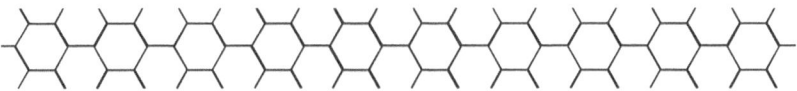

After Maude pushed the pushy salesperson out of the dressing room, Hilde put her phone back to an ear and went back to listening to the Homes Sweet Homes lawyer in Washington drone on about that silly ongoing congressional investigation. What a fool. She had already explained that not more than twenty-four hours prior to her departure from the IRS, her computer had suddenly caught fire. There could be no surviving records of her dealings with non-profit organizations seeking tax-exempt status, and anyway: None of them had any direct connection to her nominal husband's HSH Foundation. But the lawyer continued to tediously dwell on a "conflict of interest" and "potential criminal charges" related to a certain application. What did it matter? The plumbers union, backed by a corrupt Republican Senator from New Jersey, was the conflicted guilty party in the case the legal fussbudget dwelt on—for lobbying on behalf of the Privies for the Underprivileged Association—a clearly _for_ profit so-called charity that by sheer coincidence was in competition with HSH to build an affordable housing project in Newark.

Told by the lawyer—billing his overpriced time to HSH by the millisecond—that her husband, Buddy, may have fled the country, Hilde ended the call and turned to Maude. "Can't we move up the date of the Mayoral election?" she asked her slow-footed campaign manager. "The sooner I can get into a high office with executive privileges, the better."

"First things first," her trusted advisor again advised. "We need to make a few refinements to your, uh, message before re-launching your campaign." But the so-called women's fashion store, Miss Margaret's, didn't carry pantsuits in any size or color.

Though eager to move on, Hilde thought it prudent to leave the store by way of a fire exit. Maude cracked open a doorway to the exterior and peered out. Hilde put on dark glasses, then scurried to Maude's parked car. She couldn't effectively re-launch her run for high office until she had replenished her wardrobe and coordinated color of her eyes. "Maybe you lost your blue contact lens when cooking that casserole," said her persistently inquisitive friend from the driver's seat beside her, "or in the shower." Hilde didn't trust Maude enough to confess that one of her blue eyes had likely got washed down the drain of Jonathan Henry's hot trough.

"What did that nosy little reporter want?" she asked. "Could she possibly have come across a leftover, unedited copy of *Squab/1965*?"

"Possibly, but I doubt it. Those of all our classmates living locally are accounted for, except one, though some old Fighting Hens have moved out of town or died. But little Miss Henryetta is onto something, no doubt. Why else would she have tracked us up here to Fiddler's Green?"

"What dirt do we have on her?" Hilde asked. "Her name is too weird to be coincidental? She's sure to have her nose out of joint. No doubt she will fight to keep 'Henry' in town, so to speak."

"Yes, no doubt. But no one reads the *Weekly Herald* except for sports scores, store sales and occasional coupons. The **From Where I Sit** editorials by Harold Mixon—people refer to him as the 'Deep Stinker' — are enthusiastically ignored by everyone except perhaps a few 'good ol' boys' hanging around filling stations, who wouldn't know a voting booth lever from an axle. But tell me again, Hilde, <u>exactly</u> what did the *New York Times* reporter say to you?"

"He just hinted, not so subtly, that I should seek high office, like Virgil Carter. And… Oh yeah, he tried to trip me up with a gotcha question about someone named, uh, Gabe Goodheart."

"He must have meant 'Gaylord Goodhart', a high school football player who passed through town a few years ago. There was a scandal about him, or his daddy, and a hair dresser… No, now that I think about it, I recall our little Miss Henryetta might have been involved in some way. I'll check into it, in case we need to put the muscle on her."

At a 4 EYES 4 ONLY U optometry store in a roadside strip shopping center, a so-called "Doctor" Been examined Hilde's remaining blue contact lens. "Oh my," he said, "this bad boy — or bad girl, I should say — has been steamed up alright. That's why I always tell my patients to take off <u>everything</u> before getting into a hot bath, heh, heh. But it'll work itself back into shape. I'll Fed Ex a new, perfectly matched lens for your other eye in a day or so."

Back in the car, bound for a nearby Penny's store, Hilde was relieved that Maude did not again ask what had happened to her sky-blue outfit, one of only two pantsuits she had packed for what she had expected would be only a brief trip to Oklahoma. There simply was no reason her campaign manager needed to know she had "swapped" the loose-fitting garment as part of a confidential deal for Jonathan Henry's support. Though Jonathan had been highly complimentary of her good taste in clothes, the pants were too short for him. Surely he would never wear the unisex outfit in public. Political bedfellows, so to speak, had to trust each other to be discrete. But Maude's house dresses, though comfortable, were hardly suitable for a woman on the cutting edge of the political spotlight.

Inside Penny's, having been directed to the unisex leisure suits department... "My God," Hilde blurted, there she was again: That little, long-haired strawberry-blond newspaper snoop had obviously followed her, and now—armed with a notebook in hand—was making a brazen frontal attack. "Ms. Bottomly," she said, with an obviously false sweet smile. "If you don't mind me not respecting your privacy while you shop for your husband, I have just one question for the newspaper: Would you be open to a compromise of re-naming our town somethin' other than 'Etta'? My boss, Mr. Harold, is semi-unsettled on the matter, and Mayor Bailey has sent up a trial balloon off the record to see if 'Springfield'... "

"No, absolutely not," Hilde felt obliged to answer. "Obviously you, your boss, and our Republican Mayor have entirely missed the point of my Fiftieth Reunion Address to the nation. There is a War on Women still in progress. 'Henry' must go!"

"Hilde doesn't do ambush interviews," Maude said, yanking the impudent girl by her overly long hair, "but I have a little question for you, child: Were you or were you not involved with a certain 'Gaylord Goodhart' in the theft and destruction of a school bus? Tell the truth."

"Uh, me and Gaylord were what you might call 'involved' with one another," the little minx admitted, "and I guess you could say we were semi-involved in the school bus elopement accident too. It was part of what turned Gaylie semi-rotten..." The little hussy went on to tell, without a spec of shame, a bizarre story about how this Gaylord character and she might have got married "after graduation," about him being charged with rape in Oklahoma, then getting sent to prison in Texas for murder, and about how she herself went down there "with a rope" to get him out. In answer to Maude asking, the little blue-eyed seductress said a *New York Times* reporter was coming to town "any day now" to write about Mr. Goodhart's upcoming marriage, presumably to her. Why on earth would the *Times* take an interest in such a tawdry tale more fit for print in the *National Enquirer*?

Hilde glanced at Maude, alarmed. Maude glanced back, clearly suspicious of what was really afoot. *The New York Times* did not make a practice of covering small town weddings of nobodies. Obviously, the *Times* reporter who had called her about the local War on Women—Borts? Sorts? Warts?—was coming to town to… what? Build her up? Or take her down? Immediate re-launch of her campaign for Mayor in defense of the larger women's cause for gender justice was urgent!

Though unable to coordinate colors through her dark glasses, or barely even check sizes of the displayed garments, Hilde frantically snatched three or four leisure suits from a rack and bolted for a store exit as fast as her chubby legs would carry her.

IV

STOP IN THE NAME OF LOVE...
THINK IT ⊙-⊙-VER-R-R/
THINK IT ⊙-⊙-VER-R-R.

Stop in the Name of Love/ The Supremes

TWENTY ONE

On her way to the P's-n'-Q's pool hall and quaint cafe, to have lunch with her mother, Henryetta was struck by how many political signs had got put up on Main Street storefronts. Stranger still was that almost all the local business proprietors seemed to be supporting both *Mayor*—a/k/a Booster Bailey— and *I Am Woman!*—a/k/a Ms. Bottomly. She couldn't even see into the hardware store for all the red and blue thumbs on yellow posters and female symbols on light purple backgrounds plastered to the front window. Same for the Bunkhouse Motel, where... Land sakes alive! She had never known the swimming pool, stuck in the crotch of the L-shaped motel building, to have any water in it. Ordinarily, only a few older folks would just set around the edges of the empty concrete hole, sunbathing theirselves. But now, not even Summer no more, the pool was full of both bluish water and brown-skinned younguns, splashing, whooping and hollering. If her mother had not sounded so agitated on the phone, Henryetta would have gone on into the motel office to find out what in tarnation was goin' on.

Sure enough, Wynona Sue was already set down at a table, and with a glass of white wine in front of her. Ordinarily, her mother didn't drink wine with lunchtime sandwiches, except on special occasions. "Honey, set down and brace yourself," she said, which Henryetta did. "An hour ago, a very sophisticated woman, obviously from Dallas—wearing a pantsuit but otherwise stylish—came into the Hair House, wanting a trim and touch-up, or so she said, but… " Wynona Sue took a big gulp of white wine. "She let slip—brace yourself, Henryetta—Gaylord Goodhart's big same-sex wedding must have been called off, which is just as well because I have yet to find the right dress. And that's not all." Her mother took another gulp, and before Henryetta could get grip on her own wits…

"The woman from Dallas got to asking all about you! You, Henryetta, you your own self. She played coy, but I, along with Pearl and Crystal, sniffed a hint of 'other wo… other love interest' in the air, and soon got the true skinny out of her. Henryetta, I told you so: Gaylord Goodhart is coming to town on bended knee, to make an honest woman of you!"

What?! With her heart aflutter, Henryetta signaled to a waiter. If what her mother said was even semi-correct, today really was a special occasion.

"Don't lose your head, honey," her mother advised. "You know how Gaylord was always so easy to be led along by his daddy, Coach Cecil. So, please, Henryetta, don't set a date too early for me to find a dress. I have always dreamed of a Christmas Eve wedding," said Wynona Sue—with a familiar "dreamy" look in her eyes—and to a waiter who came to the table: "Make it a double."

Though not hungry anymore—plus eager as a new bride to get back to her desk and Google for reliable news about any official change in Gaylord's wedding plans— Henryetta tried to moderate her excitement.

"I always knew Cecil felt terrible about running that dang bus into a ditch," her mother said, "and not mainly because he lost his football coaching job. He never said anything. Cecil never was able to face me at all. Men are like that: shy about saying they're sorry. It has taken Cecil, the love of my life, all this time to get up the nerve to... . Yes, no doubt it's Gaylord's daddy who put that two-spirited boy up to coming back to you, Henryetta, as a way of breaking the ice between me and..." Her mother's eye-phone buzzed, she took the call and... "Oops, I did it again," she said, "and Miz Parker's head was already medium well done when she came in."

Henryetta promised her departing mother she would call later, "to talk about dresses," then floated out of the P's-n'-Q's on a cloud.

Ay, ay, ay, ay/ canta y no llores/ Porque cantando se alegran/ cielito lindo, los corozones...

She hardly noticed that the crowd in and around the Bunkhouse Motel swimming pool had grown to include lots of brown-skinned grown-ups along with youguns.

Ay, ay, ay, ay/ pajaro que abandona/ cielito lindo, su primer nido...

That a mariachi band was lined up on the pool's low diving board, strumming musical instruments and singing, seemed only as should be the case on such a special occasion

Ay, ay, ay, ay/ Una flecha en el aire/ cielito lindo, lanzo Cupido/ Ay, ay, ay, ay...

Henryetta had always known Gaylord Goodhart was, and always would be, the love of her life.

Ay, ay, ay, ay...

TWENTY TWO

Doggone it, a little Mexican boy urinated on his leg. That was what pushed Buford over the lines he had drawn around himself in the sand. Prior to that particular border incident, he had remained calm, even when an eighteen-wheeler took out the town's picket fence within sixty seconds of its erection across eastbound Interstate 40, and outran police pursuit all the way to the Arkansas state line. No telling how many illegals were hidden in the refrigerated load, but that was horse meat out of the barn, so to speak. Undeterred, he had carried on with his Mayoral duties at a command post beside the highway at its exit ramp onto the Indian Nation Parkway. From there, he had observed Chief Potter wave over at least some of the vehicles identified as suspicious by another local cop back at the interchange on the west side of town. In addition, he himself had handed out flyers to the *padres* of brown-skinned families—warning in bright red: *BIENVENIDO A AMERICA!* —and directing them by Spanish words and a map to either turn around and return to Mexico or go directly to the Bunkhouse Motel on Main Street.

But then, doggone it... The little *el nino*, not more than five or six-years-old, had got out of a van, looked up to him with an innocent seeming sparkle in his black eyes, and... Game on!

Already dissatisfied with Potter's lackadaisical attitude in the face of enemy fire, Buford had sent the Chief back to headquarters to oversee paperwork. He himself, armed with a bullhorn and small Mexican flag from the Walmart, had assumed hands-on command of the operation, dubbed "Save the Blondes." Last night, as instructed by Mr. Henry, he had read Miss Ann Coulter's book, *Adios America*, cover to cover, so he was loaded for bear. In less than an hour he sent dozens of potential Hispanic rapers and their families without papers directly to jail. To stem the unrelenting tide of unwashed humanity, he had also radioed police personnel manning the town's western border check-point to do the same. Passersby in the opposite lanes of the highway slowed down too, also stuck their heads out of car and truck windows, and yelled curses — at the Mexicans, no doubt, but...

A black-and-blue Oklahoma Highway Patrol car, with siren blaring and lights flashing, skidded to a halt on the highway shoulder. A state trooper jumped out of the vehicle. "What the f**k do you think you're doin'!" said the red-faced fellow law enforcement official.

A drop of urine may have trickled down one of Buford's legs. He shook it off. Having had the foresight to bring along his own Smokey Bear hat from his Boy Scout days, and a shined-up Kiwanis Club Junior Police badge from his grade school hitch in traffic control, Buford stood brim-to-brim, badge-to-badge with the highway patrolman and shouted, in a voice that came out high-pitched: "I am Officer Buford P. Bailey, the duly elected Mayor of Henryetta, Oklahoma. This highway runs right through our city limits. Under state law, I am authorized to uphold order within this jurisdiction, and according to Miss Ann Coulter... "

"Not if you're running a speed-trap!" the still red-faced

trooper shouted back, in a still manly voice. "You've got traffic darn near stopped dead-still all the way back to Pottowatomie County! Now get off the road and raise taxes on your own darn residents to pay your darn salary."

Aha, obviously the state cop was a Democrat, one of those on the far left that Miss Ann had warned were turning America into a third world hell hole. This little dust-up was about nothing but politics as usual. Buford stepped back. "Please, fellow officer, let's be reasonable and try to reach a compromise," he said. "If you will meet me half way, go into town and start taking these wetbacks off our hands, I will call off my police dogs for a cooling off period. Tomorrow or next week or the week after, we'll work out a comprehensive plan to... " Buford heard sirens in the near distance, the whack-whack-whack of helicopters directly overhead. All of a sudden, he found himself surrounded by television cameras and shouting reporters.

"Sheriff... " what about this?

"Sheriff... " what about that?

"Sheriff," they continued to shout, before throwing questions at him like rotten tomatoes aimed at an unfunny clown, but... It dawned on Buford that the Sheriff position was a county post, bigger and better than County Commissioner. Somewhat surprised to already be pegged for higher office, he stepped into the circle of television news people who must have raced all the way from Oklahoma City and Tulsa to cover him. "Please, please remain calm," he said, turning two thumbs downward. "I will answer your questions one by one, beginning with identification of myself as the Honorable Buford P. Bailey. "

"How do you know who to arrest?" someone yelled. "Are you engaged in racial profiling?"

"Absolutely not. I personally identify SWOPS by condition of their vehicles, and as for skin color... "

"SWOPS? What are SWOPS?"

"It's a police term for 'Spics Without Papers'. Some of the occupants of broken-down vehicles, well, earlier today, I sent a whole family of redheaded SWOPS to our new Bunkhouse jail. We wave through commercial trucks and newer cars, most of which have darkened windows so that you can't even see who's inside them."

"Ann Coulter and Donald Trump say Latino men are rapists," a brownish-skinned female reporter yelled, before going on to holler a speech about how "gringos" should be more understanding and respectful of the cultured ways of others. "The age of consent in Mexico is twelve," she said.

Buford already knew that, having read Miss Ann's book, and also knew SWOPS were not only rapers. "They are also litterers," he informed the circle of reporters. "There are so many white plastic sacks all over the ground south of the Rio Grande River, they are called the 'Mexican National Flower'. Mistletoe is Oklahoma's official State Floral Emblem, we hang it over doors at Christmas, so you can see the different cultural... "
Loud static erupted from the police radio clipped to Buford's belt. Then: "MAY DAY! MAY DAY! MAY DAY! Return to Bunkhouse immediately! I repeat: Return to jail house ASAP!"

Buford ran to his rusty old station wagon, peeled off the duct tape holding it's driver-side door shut — and with a caravan of TV station vans following in the dust behind him — sped toward the town's new jail, worried sick that a Mexican raper must have got at Ms. Wheeler or another one of the female jail clerks, even though none of them were blonde. Instead, upon his arrival at the Bunkhouse...

La, la, la, bamba/ La, la, la, bamba/ Baa-baa-bamba/ Baa-

baa-bamba/ Baa-baa-bamba...

"Mayor Bailey, thank God you're here," said Ms. Wheeler. "We are plum out of food. Taco Bueno, and not even the Chair Crushers Cafe will make another delivery without promise of immediate payment. Neither will the liquor store. And over there," she said, pointing, "on the diving board..."

Yo no soy marinero/ Yo no soy marinero/ Arriba y arriba/ y arriba, y arriba...

"...he's not raping her. Planned Parenthood told them if they did it here, they would welcome their unborn baby into the American marketplace."

La, la, la, bamba/ La, la, la, bamba/ Baa-baa-bamba/ Baa-baa-bamba/ Baa-baa-bamba...

Buford waded into the melee, and struck an arms up/ don't shoot pose, with both thumbs pointed down. "Please, please, calm yourselves," he shouted. "Please, please, *amigos,* you are disturbing the peace and quiet of your neighbors. Please, please... "

Para bailar la bamba/ Para baillar la bamba/ Se necessita una poca de gracia/ Una poca de gracia...

A blow from behind knocked Buford into the swimming pool. Though sure he was about to meet his Maker underwater, he struggled to the surface, only to be hit in the face by another misaimed burst from the fire department's water cannon. Thankfully, he survived. Thankfully, the wild jungle music had come to a halt.

By the end of the day, Buford had maxed out his Master Card to feed the hungry masses, and on his own—Chief Potter had decided to take advantage of accumulated vacation time—he had done his best to disburse the mob of Mexican detainees. But dang it, most of the potential rapers and families refused to check out of the Bunkhouse jail, much less go back home, or even continue on their way to New York. Tired and hungry himself, anxious to return to the peace and quiet of his bungalow... Buford felt a tug on a leg of his barely dried out pants, looked down and... "No! No!" he screamed. "Down, boy! Down... "Thank God, the little Mexican lad looking up to him with black puppy-dog eyes was not the same disrespectful rascal who had pissed on his leg hours earlier.

He shooed away the brown-skinned *el nino*, but... For crying out loud, the kid seemed to be part of a family of late arrivals, who had come to the Bunkhouse voluntarily. From a semi-youngish, semi-American speaking mother of the boy and a little sister—holding one of his flyers—he was able to dope out that they and a grandpa and grandma were out of gas and out of *dinero*, tired and hungry, and of course there was no room for them in the Bunkhouse.

Buford knew his mother had never been especially proud of him. His older brother, Rex, was handsomer and always got the best chow. His older sister, Ginger, was not pretty, but a quick learner who won a bunch of red ribbons for being second best. He was the runt of the litter, and even his mom used to say—only semi-joking—that no one would take little 'Bufie' off her hands. Though having been married to a Mayor, she was not particularly impressed that her youngest had also gone into politics at an early age, and had never understood that he didn't much care for animals. They lived not far apart, but he visited her only at Christmas, or when she needed something heavy brung to her. So now, upon arriving on her front porch, he dreaded knocking on his mother's door, disturbing her dogs that he heard yapping inside, and looking for a hand-out. His mom opened the door a crack.

"What is it now, Bufie?" she said. "You should know I don't like bein' bothered during *Hannity*."

Buford apologized for intruding, and explained that he had picked up a carload of "strays," but had no edible food in his bungalow, and no room to keep the pathetic creatures overnight. His mom opened the door a little wider and, dang it, shined a bright flashlight at his station wagon and squinted through her thick glasses. She loved dogs, but had no use for... "There's five garbage cans of chow out back," she said. "Scoop out what you need from the one marked with one star, but don't take none of that five-star *Grandma Lucy's Freeze-Dried Goat*. If *Old Yeller* was good enough for you, I reckon it'll do for your strays." Buford was floored by his mother's unexpected generosity. "But I'm having my dog houses redecorated right now, you'll have to make room for those you've rounded-up at your place," she added. "And anyway... "

Buford was re-floored when his mom reached out and touched his cheek. "Bufie," she said, "it's time you started a family of your own. I'm not gonna be here to take care of you forever."

TWENTY THREE

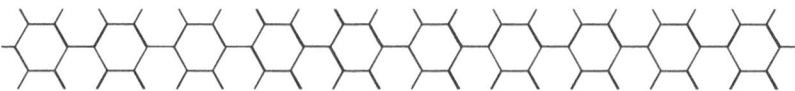

After not finding a spec of news online about any cancellation of Gaylord's wedding plans, Henryetta had come down with a cold to go with her achy heart. At home in her singles-only Shangri-La apartment yesterday afternoon, mainly watching television shows, she'd decided the notion that Gaylie would be coming back to court her likely amounted to nothing but beauty parlor gossip, probably set off by her mother's own fantasy. Wynona Sue's favorite TV show was called *Say Yes to the Dress*. She set on the divan pert near every night, sipping Friendly Creature highballs while watching gals, and their mamas, pick out expensive wedding costumes, no doubt dreaming that Coach Cecil Goodhart—or just about any man—would give her a second chance at saying yes to a wedding outfit of her own. So Henryetta didn't blame Wynona Sue for mixing things up. Instead of moping more about it all, she had just pulled up her socks and come to work, hoping to find that Benjamin Bortz would be coming to town, but...

After parking her Checker in the alley and coming in the backdoor of the *Weekly Herald* office, all she found waiting for her was Mr. Harold at his desk, and on her desk nothing but another draft of one of his editorials that was to go, finally, on the front page of this week's paper. Without much hope of noticing any powerful effect, Henryetta read:

From Where I Sit, *SAY NO TO THE DRESS*: *Change is the only constant condition we experience. I know that. (See my endorsement of altering the town name in* **Where I Sit** *to the left.) I also recognize that as folks like me get up in age, they tend to view change as generally for the worse. For old men such as myself, increasing dislike for alterations in the world we live in — as opposed to the good old days of our youth — may be Nature's way of easing our passage into an otherworldly human condition, meaning dead and gone. But I worry for my children and grandchildren. And as the cliche goes, just because you're paranoid doesn't necessarily mean everyone is not out to get you. Call me crazy, but I, for one, believe this is currently the case. And in these times of unprecedented flux in American values and personal behavior, I see the most sudden and extreme hell-in-a-handcart movement as glorification of homosexual lifestyle at the expense our traditional concept of marriage. Thankfully, here in our own little town...*

Henryetta put down the feeble blast of buckshot fired by the right-hand side of her boss' double-barrel pencil. It was dreadful unlikely to kick up any dust about any ol' Main Street statue of Gaylord, in or out of a wedding dress, especially with about everyone so stirred up about the town name and mascot. And not likely to help Benjamin Bortz get his newspaper boss to send him down to cover the story, along with the local battle in a so-called War on Women. Her prospects — not for getting married — just to have a little romance in her life, had boiled down to... Lo and behold, Benjamin Bortz's number showed up on her buzzing eye-phone.

"Yo," he said. "That sure enough is a hotbed of politics down there, Henryetta. Your 'little ol' hometown' is all the talk on this afternoon's cable news. The big story almost got me knocked out of my Oklahoma assignment by a senior writer. How come you didn't tip me off about your Mayor's latest foray into national politics?"

Foray into national politics? Henryetta seldom watched cable news shows. She had no idea what Benjamin was talking about, but had her ears perked up to hear more about his mention of having an Oklahoma assignment. "I reckoned the Mayor's foray wouldn't amount to much," she answered. "In fact, Mayor Bailey's current foray into local politics ain't even goin' so well."

"Are you kidding? They're calling your Mayor the new 'Sheriff Joe', so the national media will be coming down there in droves to build him up and tear him down."

Sheriff? The thought of "Thumbs" Bailey armed with a gun made Henryetta shudder.

"I might already be too late to get a motel room in town," Benjamin said, with what might have been an extra little bit of twinkle in his voice. "Should I look for something north, in, uh, Okmulgee, or all the way east to… "

"I reckon I can find a hotbed for you right here in town," Henryetta blurted, which must have been one of those Freudian slip-ups, she also immediately reckoned. Benjamin just laughed, and without thanking her for the invitation — or saying anything more about what Mayor Bailey had done to get his big red face on cable news — told her he would arrive in town on Thursday and — at least — that he looked forward to seeing her.

Excited as all get out, Henryetta swiveled around to face Mr. Harold, who had been quietly setting at his own desk, no doubt anxious as a wallflower for her to be impressed by his double-barrel editorials, or maybe just finally noticing her hair extensions. "I like your new hairdo, Henryetta," he said. "The

Missus used to keep hers long like that. Now she just tags along with me to the barbershop, and gets her hair styled about the same as as mine. After awhile, couples are hard to tell apart, one from the other. Nature's way, I expect." Henryetta flashed back to Gaylord's hair and hers being about the same length in high school, then returned to the present.

"Mr. Harold, haven't you heard the news," she said. "Mayor Bailey has made a dern fool of hisself again about somethin', and got national attention on the town for doin' it."

"Dang!" said her boss. "That dern statue... "

"No, I reckon the news is not about Gaylord, and not about no War on Women neither. It's gotta be a much bigger story to be put on cable news, and is happening right under our noses while we... I say cancel at least that one barrel of powerful editorial about dresses," she advised. "No need to draw national attention to Gaylord Goodhart's unnatural inclination, nor to any role his high school girlfriend might have had in nurturing it."

With Mr. Harold's jaw still dropped, Henryetta headed for the door, feeling like she had just then survived a close call. What fool thing could Mayor Bailey have done to almost knock Benjamin Bortz out of his trip to her little ol' hometown?

TWENTY FOUR

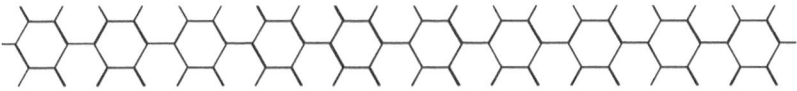

The Jonathan stepped out of his penthouse elevator and started across the Bunkhouse lobby. From out of nowhere, Bailey grabbed hold of the fringed tail of his rawhide jacket. "Mr. Henry, Mr. Henry, please, we need to talk," the wimpy Mayor said. Outside on the curb, he gave in to Bailey's man-crush and told him to get in the front seat of his SUV with Tonto. Off they went, riding ol' "Silver." But Bailey, on his knees in the front seat, facing the rear, immediately commenced to complain—believe it or not—that "Operation Save the Blondes" was too much of a success: "Even at an *AARP* Shriner convention room rate, costs of detaining Mexican rapers has already about bankrupted the town," he claimed. "There are too many of them," he whined, "and, my God, the room service charges, with mandatory tips: I never figured on any of that when I signed the lease." So what? A deal was a deal. "But Mr. Henry, you've let that... that Bottomly woman put her signs on your properties next to... some of them on <u>top</u> of my thumbs. And I threw in a hand-tooled boot to boot."

So what? He had not given either candidate exclusive signing rights. That was not the way The Jonathan rolled. He had no respect for a guy not smart enough to speed-read the sixty pages of fine print in standard commercial property leases put in front of him. "Look, Bailey, the Feds will be along any day now to take the wetbacks off the town tab. The rapers will get the message and stop coming, just like the *AARP* Shriners. Believe me, Bunkhouse occupancy will drop off; it always does when people get tired of motel food. In the meantime, just have the female guests reduce your overhead by cleaning their own rooms, doing their own laundry, lending a hand in the kitchen. Senoritas without papers say to me all the time: 'Thank you, Senor Henry, we love scrubbing floors and toilets.' They think I'm amazing, absolutely incredible. And by the way, just think how grateful Miss Ann will be to me for makin' you build that fence."

But he could see Bailey was a loser, too dense to understand a really great motivational speech when he heard one. By the time they got out to the dirt road on the south side of the JAH Ranch, his pitiful tenant had turned away, curled himself into a a ball against the front door of the SUV, and sunk into a sulky pout, just like . . "No! I don't care what I promised to do," the suddenly uncurled little kitty cat mewed, on his knees again, facing the back seat, pouting. "The deal is off, and as for having your way with a big *JAH*-branded erection on Kellogg's Korner, forget it! I want to go home."

Just like What's-Her-Name said fifty years ago, after the Senior prom, Jonathan recalled. They were parked on this very same road in his daddy's Cadillac, and... It dawned on Jonathan that Bailey was a complete sissy, a lot like... Oh yeah, his first wife was that cute little blonde, Cissy Golightly.

"Tonto!" Jonathan barked, "stop the car." To the little sissy, in a gentle but firm tone: "Fine, you want to go home: Get out and walk. That's the deal."

Five minutes later, after hobbling along the dirt road for

not even a hundred yards, with Silver cruising slowly beside him, "Wait!" the girly Mayor cried. Tonto stopped the vehicle. Jonathan opened a rear door. "Okay, okay, I'll do it," his latter day prom date said, climbing into the back seat. "Only for the good of the town," he added. "A couple of years from now, tax revenues from your hotel-and-casino venture will make the town rich." Almost just like the other Cissy said after the prom, Jonathan recalled, except she was the one who made him get out and walk after he told her he didn't have a condom handy, then let him back in the Caddy when he foolishly wavered in their negotiation of a conditional pre-nup that he had written on the palm of his hand. Later, he had to pay out even more to get her to sign a confidentiality agreement, restricting her from ever claiming she had gotten the best of him.

With the current sweetheart deal re-consummated, Jonathan dropped off Bailey at his run-down Mayor's office, feeling not fully satisfied... Not even when "Sissy" returned with his other hand-tooled boot. Still itchy, Jonathan told Tonto to take him out to Kellogg's Korner. On the way there, he congratulated himself for nailing a nice piece of business. In the past twenty-four hours, he had made more money out of his flagship Bunkhouse than over the last ninety days. And a few weeks from now, he would have the ultimate satisfaction of getting at Merlene's little patch of... What the hell?! Jonathan was startled from his semi-wet dream by the sight of no fewer than two dozen mobile houses set up along the frontage of Kellogg's Korner. Before Tonto had brought Silver to a full stop, he bolted out the rear door of the SUV and charged into the recently plowed field behind the abandoned service station building. Merlene's no-account boy, Bart, looked up, saw him coming and met him halfway across the upturned turf.

"Well, well, not even a green bud out of the ground, and you're settin' up to make wine, I see," Jonathan said to his ornery offspring. "Take my advice, boy, don't count on stomping on any grapes 'til you get 'em off the vine. Overhead like you've got going out here will eat up any chance of making a profit."

"Oh, you mean the mobile homes," the hopelessly unbusinesslike young man said. "The government has tens of thousands of them, completely unused, left-over from the Katrina disaster. FEMA is paying us to put 'em here."

Jonathan couldn't help being slightly impressed. Maybe he had misjudged the lad. And no maybe about it, he himself could and would make a better deal with Uncle Sam and get the mobile houses put in storage up on his untilled farmland, along with thousands more.

"And the Homes Sweet Homes Association is going to pay us even more money, starting tomorrow when the migrant workers start moving in."

"Migrant workers?"

"Mexicans mainly. They are sick of staying at your motel, literally. The food is inedible, they say. So Aunt Maude—she runs HSH—got the idea of moving them over here. More houses are due to arrive next week."

Damn the government! What gave politicians and bureaucrats the right to use taxpayer money to compete with hard working businessmen trying to eke out a profit?! "Take my advice, boy: You start suckin' on that government tit, you'll never be a man!" Nothing chafed Jonathan more than a healthy young male with not enough sand to stand up on his hind legs.

Back at the penthouse, with a phone to his ear... *buzz...* *buzz... buzz... buzz... buzz... buzz...* For crying out loud, no wonder the country was being overrun by Mexicans... *buzz...*

buzz... buzz... buzz... buzz... buzz... FEMA was supposed to stand for Federal Emergency Management Agency... *buzz... buzz... buzz... buzz... buzz... buzz...* "Brownie" had not done such a great job down in New Orleans, in Jonathan's opinion... *buzz... buzz... buzz... buzz... buzz...* If he were President, whoever was now in charge of FEMA would have been fired fifteen buzzes ago, but... *buzz... buzz... buzz... buzz... buzz... buzz... buzz... buzz... buzz... buzz... buzz... buzz...*

Later, as Jonathan eased himself into the hot trough... "Damnit!" During his soaking the other night with that pleasingly plump gal, Little Beaver, she must have sat her big be-hind on his clicker, and mashed it. Now the thing-a-ma-jig was stuck on the MSNBC channel that she had made him watch. He was in dire need of a good back-scratch from Miss Ann, but only a show called *The Last Word With Lawrence O'Donnell* came on the screen. A white fella, who must have been O'Donnell, sat at a table across from an Afro-American midget with a watermelon-size head, who he recognized as that sumbitch...

"Reverend Al, thanks for being here. How perfectly poetic is the justice of the latest Fox News hero, a new 'Sheriff Joe', flipping to Mother Teresa mode, turning a redneck Oklahoma town into a Sanctuary City?"

"If you're talkin' about that cracker cop assaulting that innocent, lightly armed, alleged bank robber with pepper spray inside that honky bank vault... "

"No, that's in our next segment. This is the part where you say immigration of Latino voters poses no threat to African-American employment, which is now all the way up to almost eighty-five percent, not counting teenagers and the prison population."

"Oh yeah. Republicans want to put us to back to work on

their redneck plantations: totin' dat barge, liftin' dat bale, but, uh… Hell no, we won't go. The war is about nothin' but rich whites gettin' richer by tradin' our black blood for Egyptian black gold, like black lives don't matter as much as greenbacks and wetbacks."

"Close, Reverend Al, but not quite what I am looking for at the moment. Let's try again. Some say that Mexican workers are taking unskilled jobs that would otherwise go to unemployed African-Americans. Got it? Now, what do you, the black community's go-to guy, have to say about that, just that?"

"Let 'em have all the low-pay jobs they want. We're done pickin' cotton for Whitey. We're done mowin' our own grass too. Government jobs in cities are the ones that pay decent wages, with full disability benefits from day-one, plenty of time off, and retirement at age thirty-five."

"Well said, Reverend Al. More government jobs is the only sensible way to reduce our prison population. Now, as for the cracker cop who sprayed the black Boy Scout, who was only lighting a stick of dynamite… "

Jonathan had an uneasy feeling. "Redneck Oklahoma town turning into a Sanctuary City for Mexican rapers?" Hell, that kind of thing could happen right there in Henryetta if Bailey didn't miraculously grow a pair, get off his ass and do a better job protecting the town border.

TWENTY FIVE

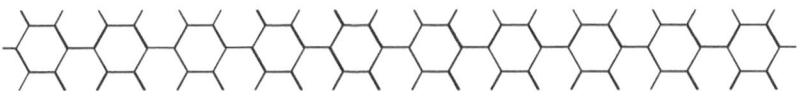

At a battery-powered candle-lit P's-n'-Q's cafe table, Henryetta continued to gaze at Benjamin Bortz, and he kept on doing about the same: glancing every other second at a mirror on the wall behind her. She couldn't necessarily blame him for admiring his own self. Except for skimpy patches of hair on his face, Benjamin looked good as a magazine cover, and smelled even better. She felt alright about her own self too. Though there were dozens of out-of-town newspeople surrounding the Bunkhouse Motel jail annex all day—covering the local angle to the illegal immigration story—she had gone back up to the Miss Margaret's store in Fiddler's Green to buy a new frock. And for almost two hours later, she'd set in her mother's beauty parlor chair, looking at a reflection of her own face in a wall mirror while Wynona Sue shined her up. Anyone who happened to walk into the pool hall and quaint cafe that night would likely take them for a cute couple, Henryetta reckoned.

But she was determined to get down to business during supper, talking with Benjamin about the big news stories that had brought him to town. He had got a room for hisself out at the Relax Inn, dang it, but she had bought a *Musky Mood* scented candle and put a six-pack of fancy designer beer in the icebox at her Shangri-La singles-only apartment. Her plan was to invite Benjamin back there later, to set on the divan next to each other, then get into personal chit-chat that might lead to, well, other personal things. But so far, all he seemed to have on his mind was...

"Soccer, it's the new gentlemen's football, not like our brutish American game played by muscled up Neanderthals," he said. "I covered Beckham lots of times, once up close and personal, after he retired from playing and came back to London. It's almost impossible for just anyone to get in Club *PucePucePuce*, but I saw him there one night, and actually got a sniff of his after-shave: *Narcissismo*. He was wearing a *Johannes Huebi* sweater, white-and-tight, over an *Our Gordon* tee-shirt, black of course, and *Dapper Dandy* banded jeans. Victoria was nowhere in sight, so I edged closer for another whiff and... "

"Our Mayor doesn't know what to do with all the Mexicans comin' into town," Henryetta said, again. "Soon as he gets a bunch checked out of the Bunkhouse Motel, along comes more of 'em, waving 'Welcome to the United States' flyers that he his own self printed up and accidentally let the wind scatter."

"...sets his *Mucho Macho* razor at exactly two-eighths of an inch, keeps his scruff exactly like mine," Benjamin continued, rubbing whiskers on his chin, that by the look of them would likely have washed off in light rain. "Men should look like men, especially in these times of gender flux, but only up to a fine point. Beckham was the first bigtime jock to demonstrate that, yeah, sweat might look like natural moisturizing from the grandstand, but *apres sport* grooming, not to mention personal hygiene, requires a lot more than a quick shower."

Henryetta tried again: "In her so-called campaign to unseat our Mayor, Ms. Bottomly has yet to say anything about illegal

Mexican infiltration bein' connected—like she says about everything else—to the Republican War on Women. But more important, from the background information I sent to you, what do you think, Benjamin? Is there anything about the name 'Henryetta', spelled with a y, that needs fixin'?"

Benjamin ignored her question and pushed his salad plate to the side. But when a waitress came to take the rest of his order, that he'd hmmed over earlier, he said he was done. Henryetta cancelled her prior selection of sweetbreads *a la Ray Ray*, but before she could ask the waitress to hurry up with the check, Benjamin leaned across the table at her, put his hands under his chin, gazed into her eyes and said: "Henryetta, let's talk about Gaylord."

He went on to say that the sports world had been in a state of denial about "rumors" of one of their heroes being gay, until announcement of Gaylord's upcoming "nuptials." Now, even real gentlemen's football fans around the world were in shock, as though the great Beckham his own self had come out of a closet, looking—and maybe smelling—"too metrosexual." The story went way beyond sports, Benjamin said, which was the reason he'd come to town. He was working on a long piece for the*Times*, and she was a big part of the big story, he said. He had in mind a whole section "explaining" Gaylord from her unique personal perspective. "I mean, for cryin' out loud, Henryetta, if not for you, Gaylord Goodhart would still be rotting in that prison down in Texas, or might have got the needle for supposedly murdering his own father." He leaned back from her and sighed.

"Henryetta, I like you, a lot, and don't want to embarrass you," he said. "I might not have to divulge your name, but the story has to be told. The public deserves all the truth fit to print. It was you who spotted Gaylord's 'daddy' in the crowd, disguised but missing a thumb, wasn't it? You are the suspected 'Oklahoma fan' who dropped that loop of rope around Cecil Goodhart, tied it to a railing and left him dangling by his neck from an upper tier of that old Texas Aggie football stadium. Right? You did it because Gaylord was the love of your life, right?"

"So what?" she replied. "Coach Goodhart didn't choke to death. They cut him down right after finishing that Aggie fight song."

Though disappointed that at the moment Benjamin Bortz was obviously more interested in a story about Gaylord than in her, well, she'd not been out on a date since Gus was a pup, so... "Gaylord Goodhart ain't the love of my life no more," she firmly stated, "but as far as telling anything from my own personal perspective, maybe we ought to go back to my singles-only Shangri-La apartment and... " She noticed Benjamin was back to looking past her, with an almost adoring look in his eyes that must have been equal to that of the famous boy in oldtime Greece, admiring a reflection of his own self in a pool of water. She turned around her head and... O-M-G. Right there in the P's-n'-Q's pool hall and quaint cafe — big as life, green-eyed and pretty as ever — stood Gaylord his own self. Henryetta like to have swooned.

"Gaylord, my pleasure, and an honor to meet you," said Benjamin, up on his feet and sticking out a hand for Gaylord to shake, before he had chance to lean down and give her a hug. "And congratulations on your upcoming, uh, induction into the Ring of Honor. Please, join us," he said, yanking a chair from another table. "Have you had dinner? We were just about to order a steak or... How about a light souffle?"

"I just came by to ask Henryetta something," Gaylord said, looking down at her in that bashful way of his. She rose up, but halfway to gettin' lips to lips... "Sit down and ask away," Benjamin said. "We're all friends here. And by the way, what's that cologne you're wearing, *Testosteroni*?"

Looking embarrassed, Gaylie admitted that he had doused hisself with *Old Spice*, "for the occasion," and looking semi-reluctant, set down. Henryetta, though wanting to climb onto Gaylord's lap and kiss him all over, couldn't think of anything to say that wouldn't have been too personal, and awkward under the circumstances. "Howdy" and such was about all that came out of her mouth, and when Benjamin commenced to jabber, the romantic mood of their reunion seemed to pass. Listening to Benjamin's questions, mainly about what it was like for Gaylord to be a "culture idol"—and the "idol" answering mainly with "I dunnos," a few "Yeps," and a lot of "Nopes"—Henryetta thought it would have been hard for an eavesdropper, such as her own self, to know which of them was reputed to be gay.

During more than an hour of that two-way "conversation," she plotted how to get rid of Benjamin Bortz, and get Gaylord onto the divan in her Shangri-La singles-only apartment. Finally getting at the matter in a ladylike manner, she yawned and casually asked Gaylie if he had a place to stay for the night. Just as she had hoped, and expected, he said he hadn't thought "that far ahead." Whoopee! But before she could grab him by an ear and drag him out of the P's-n'-Q's, Benjamin had him by an arm, practically lifting him out of his chair, telling her to run along and "get her beauty rest." She rose up and yanked at Gaylord's other arm, but... "I have an extra king-size bed in my motel room," Benjamin insisted, "and a *Beau Brummel* portmanteau fully stocked with men's essentials. We have a lot to talk about, don't we Gaylord. You two can catch up on personal chit-chat in the morning, or... Henryetta, why don't you come over and join us. The Relax Inn is bound to have a sauna."

Poor, dear Gaylord, always easily led, at least protested that he needed to talk to her about something personal in the morning, but allowed hisself to be took to the Relax Inn. Poor, pathetic her, started for her Shangri-La singles-only apartment alone, but with her heart aflutter about what Gaylord Goodhart aimed to ask her, finally, in only about twelve more hours.

FOOLS' NAMES AND FOOLS' FACES OFTEN APPEAR IN PUBLIC PLACES. 10/23/15

*Barbara Bush, Public Bathroom Wall/
Exxon Station/ Queens, New York*

TWENTY SIX

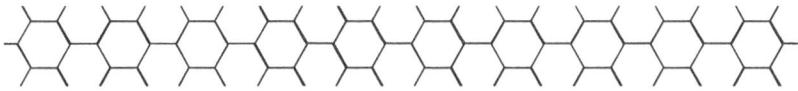

In an early morning dither, Hilde tried to prepare herself for re-launch of her Mayoral campaign, but... "Damit!" A new contact lens sent by that quack optometrist, "Doctor" Been at the 4 EYES 4 ONLY U store, was not perfectly matched with her blue lens; it was imperfectly as brown as her already brown left eye. And the leisure suits she'd hurriedly snatched off a rack in the unisex department of the out-of-town Penny's store, while wearing sun glasses... "Damnit!" They were bright orange, and had an unflattering college slogan—***RIDE 'EM!***—printed in black across the rear, as well as *OSU Cowboys* logos on both of two large breast pockets. Now, after putting on sun glasses again, she was barely able to read, much less grasp, the list of talking points Maude had typed for her second maiden appearance on the local political scene. "Just relax and be yourself," Maude advised from beside her, as they entered the Henryetta Middle School. "This is just a warm-up. Current members of the Girls Hobbies Class can't even vote in the election."

Hilde sighed. The students might not be allowed to vote in the immediately upcoming Mayoral election, alas, but one of her first acts in office would be to issue an executive order reducing the voting age of consent to twelve, only for girls, who were smarter than males and matured earlier. Inside a classroom, "Class! Class! Class!" shouted a male instructor, while wiping grime on his already dirty apron. "Turn off your blow torches and listen-up!" He then mis-introduced her as "Officer Bottom" and said she was there to "offer a few tips," not on breaking through the glass ceiling of the patriarchal world his young female students had been born into, but on "how to get out of a steel cage."

Though not exactly sure of what the practical purpose of such instruction might be, Hilde intuitively identified with the vivid imagery. Without thinking, she took off her sun glasses. Involuntarily, her brown eye began to blink. Perhaps concerned that she had gotten a spark of something in her lensless eye, the instructor offered her a pair of thick yellow goggles. She put them on and proceeded with her rehearsed opening remarks, intended to warm this particular audience to her:

"You know, I well remember," she said, forcing a smile, "when I was a girl about your age... "

"What, are you an elephant?" someone said in a muffled voice from behind a full-face, metal welder's mask. Only slightly ruffled, "Oh no, I am not a Republican," Hilde answered, with a practiced chuckle. "I am a donkey."

"Yeah, a big jackass!"

Ha, ha, ha...

Slightly more unsettled by the unexpectedly timed burst of laughter, Hilde continued: "When I was your age, I began my lifelong fight for women's rights. To this day, unlike our current Mayor, I am Woman!"

"Had me fooled!"

Ha, ha, ha...

She pressed on: "Take the minimum wage, for instance: It's a women's issue."

"You take a minimum wage. I'm gonna be a welder."

"Good for you," Hilde answered, with regained composure and practiced smile. "You know, Rosie-the-Riveter, like myself, was a woman who learned how to 'blowtorch' herself out of a steel cage."

The class instructor raised his hand. "Rosie O'Donnell might be a riveter, and might have escaped from the slammer, but Rosie's no woman, Ms. Bottom," he volunteered. "You must be thinking of Lawrence O'Donnell."

Hilde soldiered on, ticking off women's issue after women's issue, from undocumented immigration to same-sex marriage. Building up to a fiery finale demanding change of the town name and mascot, however, she noticed Maude frantically signaling to her with a throat-cutting gesture. "In closing," Hilde said, "suffice it to say: I deserve to hold high office because I am woman!"

"Prove it!"

"Show us what you got behind those OSU patches!"

"Shake your booty for us, Officer Big Bottom!"

Hilde, mouth agape, took off the yellow goggles to make a two-eyed, brown-and-blue death stare at the rude adolescent girls. They lifted their welders' masks and...

Ha, ha, ha, ha, ha, ha, ha, ha, ha, ha...

My God, the middle school students in attendance were all pimply-faced males!

Ha, ha, ha, ha, ha, ha, ha, ha, ha, ha, ha...

In horror, she fled from the classroom. Hurrying down a hallway, she passed by a door clearly signed *Girls Hobbies Class*. What a clusterf**k! And none of it was her fault!Retreating from the political battlefield in Maude's hopelessly out-of-date car, Hilde berated her inept campaign manager for not vetting the chosen audience for her foray into the hustings. "Your ad lib jokes went over well," Maude replied, in feeble defense of her own gross mismanagement of the campaign re-launch. "And Hilde," she said, with a shamefaced sideways glance from behind the wheel of her jalopy, "sooner or later you are going to have to take your message to the broader electorate, which includes adolescent males of voting age, many well past fifty. Let's stop on Main Street and do some eye-to-eye, man-to-man campaigning. National news media were swarming around the Bunkhouse Motel detention center yesterday, to cover 'Sheriff' Bailey. It's a good opportunity for you to re-launch and... "

"Absolutely not!" Hilde answered, as they turned onto the town's Main Street. "And by the way," she said, "why are Bailey's thumb signs still stuck on Jonathan Henry's buildings? For cryin' out loud, is it the candidate's job to sneak around at night and take them down! Do I have to do everything? Where are all the volunteer Hilde Helpers?"

"Uh, everyone, at least all of us Fighting Hens, are fired up by your bold initiative to re-name the town for one of our own kind, Hilde, but, uh, no one has volunteered to help you get elected Mayor. Not even the local Democratic hacks, or their wives. We need to, uh, make you more, uh, likable. Maybe a tea at the house. I'll get out some doilies and... "

What a ninny? If likability was what mattered in politics, that asshole—Jonathan Henry—would not have been able to pay-off the football team, and cheerleaders, to steal the Student Council election from her fifty years ago. And the dumb idea of "doilies"... Nearing the Bunkhouse Motel, surrounded by TV news cameras as well as an unruly mob shouting through bullhorns, Hilde turned away from the car window and ducked her head, unpositioned so far on many of the various causes

BOOBS

their placards proclaimed: ***BLACK LIVES MATTER… WE WANT WEED!… OCCUPY SESAME STREET*** and so on. Though many ***FIGHT FOR ETTA*** and ***FIGHT FOR THE FIGHTING HENS*** signs were also held up in front of the TV cameras, she saw not a single one proudly supporting the cause of ***I AM WOMAN!***

"Pull over at HSH headquarters, Maude. We need to re-re-launch, and fast."

Immediately after they parked and got out of Maude's car, rude persons holding cameras, microphones and pads of paper, surrounded them like flies attacking rotten fruit. "Which of you is Ms. Rouser?" one of them shouted. "Which of you is running for Mayor?" shouted another. Hilde shoved Maude onto the front line and backed away. In answer to questions about the role the Homes Sweet Homes Association had played in "turning the town into a 'Sanctuary City'," Maude stooped her shoulders, peered over the tops of her rimless spectacles, and in an enfeebled old woman's voice, explained that the Hogback Manor affordable housing project—recently relocated to Kellog's Korner and re-named "Hogback Haciendas"—had been in the works for years. "As for sales and rental of federally subsidized units to… Did you say 'illegal Mexicans', dearie? The rules don't allow us to inquire about nationality, race, creed, color or anything else, except current or intended party affiliation. First come, first serve, that's the All-American way."

"What about the Mayoral candidate from out of town, Ms. Bottomly: Isn't she the brains behind the Home Sweet Homes Foundation in Washington, and if so… ?"

"Oh no, you little rascal, Hilde <u>Bottomly</u> is connected to her husband only by marriage, and has nothing to do with his good works. She is running for Mayor strictly as an independent woman!"

"What's her position on illegal immigration? Seems the sitting Mayor wants to change the name of the town to, say, Tijuana?" That crack drew a round of applause from the news media, Hilde noted. "Ms. Bottomly is strongly in favor of a comprehensive plan to address undocumented immigration, which is essentially a women's issue, as is the town name."

"What comprehensive plan?" the obviously right-wing paparazzi yelled in unison, but her occasionally wily campaign manager now shoved Hilde, unarmed and virtually blind, completely out of the circle of enemy forces. Inside the storefront office of the local Homes Sweet Homes operation, however, her fundamentally naive so-called handler reverted in character to pathetic old "Aunt Maude," twisting a hankie in her hands and whimpering about incidental use of the premises for minor political purposes. At Hilde's demand that the HSH franchise checkbook be handed over, Maude produced an antique lace fan from a pocket of her dowdy house dress, complaining of vapors — as well as "rules" — and threatening to faint.

"F**k the rules, and the vapors," Hilde shouted. "It's my foundation. I have prostituted myself for years to fund it. And besides, Maudie," she said in a softer tone, gently taking possession of the checkbook from her franchisee, "those Mexican migrants you finagled homes sweet homes for: They and their amigos from the old country are needy for a little walking-around money."

Hilde was not to be denied. After a lifetime on her knees, sucking up to powerful men, yes, she <u>deserved</u> to be elected to high office! Taking pen in hand to write a check... her phone buzzed. It was that worry-wart of a lawyer from Washington again. Against her better, feminine instinct, she took the call. "Mrs. Moon," said the lawyer's dreary voice. "I'm afraid I have bad news, about Buddy."

TWENTY SEVEN

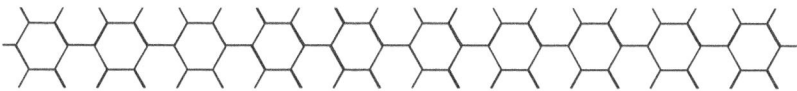

After a sleepless night, followed by an hour of waiting at the pink formica dinette table in her Shangri-La singles-only apartment, Henryetta realized she might have made a mistake. Hoping so, she put out the *Musky Mood* candle, and hightailed it in her yellow Checker over to Trudgeon Street, where her mother still lived. Praise the Lord, there set Gaylord on the front porch of her girlhood house, where he had first courted her. And Wynona Sue seemed to have already gone to work at the Hair House, which was a mercy. Back in her high school days, from questions and advice put to her by her mother, she knew dern well that Wynona Sue had been at the window, listening and maybe even watching her spark with Gaylord. "Honey, if you keep slappin' his hand, he might just quit reachin' for the candy," she seemed to recall her mother saying, or... Now that she thought about it, Henryetta reckoned it was more likely that she her own self had handed out sweet treats to Gaylord, who was always too shy to ask, much less grab.

Up on the porch, they had a little hug, then set together on a wicker love seat. "That Benny, he's a nice fella," Gaylord said. "Daddy usually does all my talking for me, but Benny was real interested to know all about my unknown mama, Daddy, and you too, Henryetta. He sure enough thinks the world of you, and said how sorry he was you would have to go to work in an office today. He's gonna pick me up at ten, to go fishin' out at Possum Pond."

Henryetta looked at her watch. Heck, it was almost ten already. And heck again, out at Possum Pond, in the back seat of her yellow Checker was where Gaylie and she used to steam up the car windows to the point Hattie wouldn't have it, and sometimes past. "Maybe you should send Benny on down to Dallas to put his questions to your daddy," she advised. "He's a big city newspaper reporter, you know, not just a nice fella who came down here to go fishin'."

"Yeah, Daddy wants to keep a lid on the can 'til everything gets settled about… Well, I guess you heard about me and Billy Ray."

Henryetta allowed as how she had heard the two of them were teammates on the Dallas Cowboys football team, but wasn't up to date on anything getting "settled" between them.

"Well, you see, the Nike clothes company is awful het up to start sellin' a new line of outfits, and wants me and Billy Ray to be their models. But Mr. Doolittle—he owns all us Cowboys—didn't put Billy Ray under as long a sentence in Dallas as Daddy got for me. So now the San Francisco Forty-Niners are tryin' to get Billy Ray to go play ball out there, and the Nike clothes company has offered them a billion dollars to change their name to the Sixty-Niners, to match the name of a new brand of clothes."

Henryetta, with her heart aflutter, began to see that Gaylord's so-called "engagement" to Billy Ray might have been nothin' more than a business arrangement all along.

"That's why Mr. Doolittle wants to put me and Billy Ray

into a Ring of Honor and get the Nike money for his own self, even though we haven't got old and retired yet like all the other Cowboys whose names are painted on a sign band around the stadium: Mr. Lilly, Mr. Staubach, Mr. Aikman, Mr. Doolittle's name of course, and some others."

Henryetta, reckoning she had heard enough about all that, looked at her watch again, but Gaylord, obviously nervous about getting to the point of his visit, kept on explaining: "Mr. Doolittle and Daddy figured out that if they put me and Billy Ray into the Ring of Honor as legally one, the Forty-Niners couldn't get at him, and together we would count as only a single roster spot. But, Henryetta, I always cared so much about you… "

Honk… Honk… Dang it, Benjamin had arrived at the curb.

"… I just don't think I can go out there into that Ring of Honor… "

Honk… Honk . . Honk…

"… with anyone but you at my side."

Honk… Honk… Honk…

They looked deep into each other's eyes, and finally…

Honk… Honk… Honk…

"Henryetta, I would be honored if you would, well, be my best man."

Honk… Honk… Honk…

Gaylord had no more than bounded off the porch, jumped in a car with Benjamin Bortz, and started down Trudgeon Street, when Wynona Sue appeared like an evil genie uncorked from a bottle, then set down on the wicker love seat.

"Well, well, well," her mother said, "best man in a Ring of Honor! What a shame, honey: You'll have to rent a tuxedo 'stead of get a new dress." Oh goody, and if Gaylord was to be the "groom," maybe Mr. Harold would cease to worry about side effects of that dern statue Mayor Bailey was set on putting up.

In her confused state of mind—still not sure Gaylord was really gay—Henryetta wasn't really all that surprised by the turn of events. Last night, tossing and turning in bed, the truth had come to her in a nightmare: Sure enough, by naming her daughter 'Henryetta', spelled with a y, her mother had put a curse on her alright. But not necessarily just to tie her to the little ol' town of the same name, spelled the same way. No, the truth was that Wynona Sue <u>wanted</u> her to be a boy!

"Why, honey, how could you even think such a thing?" the evil genie cooed. "It was your no-account Cajun daddy who was so set on havin' a little '*Henri*' to go fishin' with. And his mama, your crazy Cajun grandma, was the one who mumbled all that voodoo nonsense on the way to the hospital delivery room. You came out a girl, but it probably wasn't <u>all</u> your fault your daddy ran away."

Uncomforted by her mother's explanation, Henryetta stepped off the porch, determined to do something about her predicament. No matter what the rule book said about a news reporter not openly taking sides in political elections, she aimed to persuade Mr. Harold to write up another powerful front page editorial in favor of Ms. Bottomly for Mayor. And she her own self would speak out loud in public from where she her own self set, by pasting *I Am Woman!* signs all over her yellow Checker.

TWENTY EIGHT

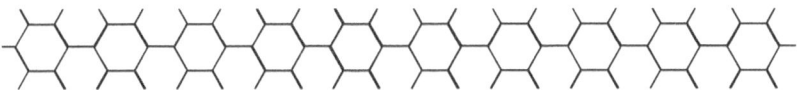

With no alarm clock beside the living room sofa, Buford might have slept 'til noon, if not for the strange aroma of something actually cooking in the kitchen of his Trudgeon Street bungalow. There, at the stove, he found the semi-youngish Maria who he had taken in night before last scrambling an egg gotten from somewhere. Mixed with *Old Yeller* and seasoned—yummy—breakfast was even more delicious than the *Grandma Lucy's Freeze-Dried Goat* served by his mother at Christmas Dinners. After getting himself ready to go to work, he saw that the semi-youngish Maria and her younguns had set to scrubbing the kitchen floor. Outside, her daddy, Hernando, was mowing grass. Her mother, also a Maria, was weeding a previously abandoned flower bed. The timing wasn't right for taking them back to their car, gassing them up and sending them back to Mexico, Buford decided. In fact, somehow his up close and personal exposure to the family of SWOPs made him feel a little uneasy about his new nickname, "Sheriff Buford," but...

In Chief Potter's absence, he owed it to the town—not to mention the national news media—to wear the badge, as well as meet his re-election responsibilities as Mayor. Upon arriving in downtown, yep, just as he had feared, all hell had broke loose during his overnight break from maintaining law and order. The Mexicans appeared to have been squeezed inside the motel jailhouse. But now, instead of a mariachi band making an infernal racket, a mob of other outsiders—pathetically drawn to the national media spotlight—held up signs in front of TV camera crews and shouted threatening slogans:

I shot the Sheriff/ I shot the Sheriff/ I shot the Sheriff...

Fight, fight, fight for the Fighting Hens!

Stand up for transgender rights! Stand up for transgender rights!

Fight, fight, fight for the Golden Knights!

Now lets' shoot the deputy...

Fight, fight, fight for Etta!

We want weed! We want weed! We want weed!

Fight, fight, fight for Henry!

I shot the Sheriff/ I shot the Sheriff...

Stand up for my right to stand up and pee! Stand up for my right to...

Steering clear of the would-be sheriff-shooters—with his badge now in his pocket—Buford got in the face of an illegal urinator. "Not in the ladies room and not in public!" he shouted, as TV camera crews circled around him like rock star groupies wanting an autograph. "And not on anyone's pantlegs," he added, before dressing down the outside agitator with a stern lecture on proper bathroom behavior. With him put in his place, Buford lifted his arms and raised two thumbs high above his head to signal victory in the even more important battle to take would-be Mexican rapers off the interstate highways of America. His junior high school student council victory speech came to mind. "Vinnie, Vicky, and Vito: I came, I saw, and... "

Fight, fight, fight for Etta!

Stand up for my rights to stand up and pee…
Fight, fight, fight for Henry!

"Sheriff Buford, are you backing down on your stand against illegal immigration?" a reporter shouted. "MSNBC says you've turned this town into a Sanctuary City."

I shot the Sheriff/ I shot the Sheriff…

Sanctuary City? Buford had no idea what the newswoman was talking about, but… "Sanctuaries are for the birds, ha, ha… Uh, but as for turning this town into a city, yes, right now I am not on liberty to publicly confide confidential details, but I will soon announce a major project out at…"

I shot the Sheriff/ I shot the Sheriff…

"Sheriff Buford, Fox News says you are setting up a permanent tent city, going one better than your law enforcement colleague out in Arizona, Sheriff Joe, in the fight to keep Mexican criminals on the edge of town?"

We want weed! We want weed! We want weed…
We want Etta!
We want Henry!

Tent city? Again, Buford was stumped, but… "City, yes, as I said, but tents… " He extended his arms and turned both thumbs down. "Details of a certain economic development initiative have to stay between me and the lamp post for now, but I can tell you that on the west edge of town, property presently known as 'Kellogg's Korner'… "

We want Etta!
We want Henry!

"You mean 'Hogback Haciendas'? Is that the major project you're talking about: affordable *casas* for illegal immigrants?"

We want weed! We want weed! We want weed…

Hogback Haciendas? Affordable *casas* for SWOPs? Before

he could respond to the unfounded rumor, no doubt started by that... that Ms. Bottomly, a jailhouse clerk rushed to Buford's side and whispered into an ear. Outraged by the awful truth of rumors undoubtedly spread by that... that woman, he broke from the circle of reporters, ran to his rusty car, and sped west on Main Street, toward Kellogg's Korner. In the rearview mirror, he saw the national news hounds were in hot pursuit. The only so-called affordable anythings he had ever approved were those cheap apartments included in a Maude Rouser project to be squeezed between Spanish mansions planned for the hogback overlooking the town's Hot Links golf course. And that economic development initiative had bit the dust long ago. Under no circumstances would he allow anyone to put cheap *casas* anywhere near the site he had committed to...

"Dang!" On the Kellogg's Korner property, right where a fifteen-story Bunkhouse Motel, casino and high-class gentlemen's club were to be built, sure enough: Mobile houses were lined-up like eighteen-wheelers in the parking lot of a low-class **XXX** roadside porn store. After skidding to a halt, then climbing out the window of his stuck car door, Buford saw out in a field beyond the box houses—"Doggone it!"— Mexicans, no doubt many of the same ones he had rounded up day before yesterday, milled around out there, free as birds of a feather. A white-skinned fella standing next to a woman wearing a Chinese hat, identified himself as the owner of the Kellogg's Korner property. Buford jerked both thumbs over his shoulders toward the rear, and told him to clear the site of his mobile houses. "They don't belong to me," the fella said. "They're owned by the Home Sweet Homes Association. Aunt Maude got federal permits from FEMA and HUD to put 'em here, at least during the humanitarian emergency in town."

Buford was stunned. Those two... those two <u>women</u>—Aunt Maude and her friend, Ms. Bottomly—had gone around his head to Washington, D.C. But, dang it, he had to admit, only to himself, that he, Buford P. Bailey, had accidentally caused the so-called "humanitarian emergency" that allowed them to do it. And if that revolting development didn't take the rag off the bush, the property owner stuck out a hand and introduced himself as none other than "Bart <u>Henry</u>!"

After staggering back to his idling car in a daze, Buford hightailed it back toward town, followed by the caravan of news channel vans. Safely inside his insurance agency think tank, he pulled down the storefront office window shade, hung the *Out to Lunch* sign on the door, and put his head on his desk. Bart Henry had to be a close relative to The Jonathan, their yellowish hair was a sure tip-off, not to mention their name. But why would the elder family member have made such a sweetheart deal—handing over the Bunkhouse Motel—to have the town take title to the Kellogg's Korner property owned by kin at a cheap price? And why would he put him, the town Mayor, up to causing a border ruckus that led to Aunt Maude and that... that Bottomly woman squatting on the planned new Bunkhouse Motel project? He'd always heard politics made strange bedfellows, but...

Buford's head popped up, clear of fog as the air around him. Jonathan Henry and that... that woman, Ms. Bottomly, obviously <u>were</u> bedfellows, which was almost too strange to imagine. Heck, Mr. Henry had let her put up signs on his properties, which was a sure tip-off they were in cahoots to... Hmmm, in cahoots to not only make him, the town Mayor, look like a dang fool, but to... Hmmm, to also put that big-bottomed Bottomly woman in <u>his</u> seat! In fact... Though Buford hated to even think such a thought, into his cleared head it came: Jonathan Henry might not really be a Republican!

Buford again put his head on the desk, this time with a thud. Back to his senses sometime later, he knew what he had to do: Clear the town of SWOPs.

He pulled back an edge of the window shade and peeked out. Satisfied that the camera crewmen had gone to lunch, he left the think tank, but inside his car, continued to think: By emptying the Bunkhouse jail and then not booking any more detainees, motel room rent owed to Mr. Henry would amount to zero, but the town would still have a permanent lease of the property—not including the penthouse, dang it—to use for offices, storage, and other public purposes. Then he would go after Maude Rouser's 'Hogback Haciendas' rats nest, by firing off a strongly worded letter to the town's Congressman in Washington, demanding that FEMA and HUD revoke the Homes Sweet Homes Association's emergency permits. But before doing all that—as Buford had learned as a boy from his mother—charity ended at home. The semi-youngish Mexican woman, Maria, along with her aged parents and young children, had to go.

From the curb in front of his bungalow, Buford couldn't help noticing how neat and tidy the property looked. Same inside, where Grandpa Hernando sat in a straight chair beside the Lazy-Boy recliner, watching TV. Grandma Maria sat on the sofa, folding towels from a pile of laundry next to her. The little boy, Pedro, ran to him, with a twinkle in his eyes and... only tugged at a leg of Buford's trousers. In the kitchen, the semi-youngish Maria and her little girl, also named Maria, stood at the table, smiling at him. A pot sat on a trivet. Buford lifted the lid and... ahh, he would have sworn it was Christmas.

In the living room after his snack, not in the mood to re-enter the national spotlight—as well as feeling overfed and in need of a brief midday *siesta* in the recliner—Buford watched a Spanish-language TV re-run of his favorite movie. After seeing the dark-skinned Amazon woman win again, he carefully considered a slight modification to his plan of action, for about two seconds. "One thumb down, one thumb up," he decided. Evicting the Mexican Maria's family and locking his bungalow doors to any future home invasion by Hispanics without papers could wait until after the election.

TWENTY NINE

Henryetta looked up from word processing a story about urination rights and saw Benjamin Bortz come through the door of the *Weekly Herald* storefront office. Out at Possum Pond all day, fishing with Gaylord, the *New York Times* reporter had missed the outbreak of culture war skirmishes that had broke out somethin' fierce. Before she could even start telling him about what was happening around the Bunkhouse Motel jail, he waved a hand to put her off and set down next to her desk. "Henryetta, this is off the record for now, but I wanted you to know what looks like the truth: Gaylord is no more gay than I am."

She stifled any little heart flutter that might have occurred by habit, as Benjamin went on to tell what Gaylord had already told her earlier: His daddy, Coach Goodhart, and Mr. Doolittle, owner of the Dallas Cowboys team, had manipulated Gaylord and Billy Ray; they had set up the Ring of Honor "wedding" to keep the two teammates from splitting up; money to be made from the Nike sports apparel-and-equipment company was behind it all. Not only had she already heard about all that, Henryetta had about washed Gaylord Goodhart—and Benjamin Bortz too—out of her extended hair, and pert near ceased to care about Gaylie's sex inclination, except to still wonder if it was something boyish about her — and her dern name — that he had cottoned to in the first place.

"I've got Gaylord under wraps at the Relax Inn," Benjamin whispered. "I'm going to drive him to Dallas and straighten him out. He's not a *Nike* brand guy, for cryin' out loud. I'm going to go around Daddy Goodhart and Dooley Doolittle before he goes through what he called called 'conformation', though he may have meant some kind of religious confirmation ritual in Billy Ray's family church. My plan is to hook-up Gaylie with *Hugo Boss*, and get him headed in the right direction. Don't worry, Henryetta, he'll be back to you in no time, good as new," he said, standing up. "Gotta go."

Henryetta knew better than to get her hopes up again about Gaylord coming back to her "good as new." And in the meantime, she had a passel of stories to write. In addition to local folks — mainly divided by their genders — making a dreadful strong fuss about "Fighting Hens" vs. "Golden Knights" and "Etta" vs. "Henryetta," all manner of unmoderated people had come into town to wave their signs and yell their complaints in front of national news reporters. Some wanted black lives to matter, some wanted China to let go of Tibet and be nice to a Dalai Llama, some even said they wanted to shoot at "Sheriff" Bailey, and so on. She had already wrote a piece about a high school classmate of hers, who wanted the Mayor to uphold his constitutional right to get free weed under Obamacare, and she still wasn't done. Henryetta brushed a hair extension off her face and went back to typing:

...self identified as a transgender person who feels like a man, carried a sign saying "Let My People Pee!" and said forcing her/him to set in a stall to urinate violated her/his constitutional rights. She/he

*wants wall-mounted "bidays" put up in public men's rest rooms so she/
he will not have to set alone in a stall like a second-class citizen, and
can "stand there like other guys and talk about weather." Not many
onlookers yelled at her/him, but when an opposite inclined him/her
went in a ladies room in the lobby of the Bunkhouse jail, Ms. Wheeler,
a regular female clerk in the police department, ran out screaming that
she had been visibly sex assaulted by sight of that transgender person's
pecker. Mayor Bailey came around later, and told the man/woman
that constitutional rights of public bathroom use would best be left a
matter of each American's personal bathroom plumbing, or maybe not.*

*As to whether curious grade school boys and mischievous high school
boys could be trusted to tell the truth about feeling like girls...*

Mr. Harold busted in, obviously in a dither. In his youth,
her boss had decided on his own that for a boy to swing his
arms when walking was to swagger, so had trained hisself to
walk in a kind of at-attention posture, which seemed to alter
any swagger into up-and-down bobbing. Now, pacing back and
forth in front of her desk, his upward bobs like to took him
off his feet. Suddenly, he stopped, turned his head and and
stared at her, like she had stole his watch or somethin'. "On top
of every thing else that's going on in town, my editorial—your
editorial, Henryetta—has stirred up a hornets nest over at the
high school," he said. "We never had a gang problem before, but
Principal Coons called me into his office and complained that
most of the girls and boys have divided themselves up as 'Ettas'
and 'Henrys.' Just imagine!"

That was nothin' exactly new, Henryetta reckoned. Back in
her own high school days, a bunch of boys had took to calling
theirselves "Phi Lambs," and another bunch, including Gaylord,
identified theirselves as "Alpha Delta Bulls." Girls formed a "Pom
Pom" gang and another group—including her own self—took

to calling theirselves the "Tom Toms." Now, girls vs. boys…

"Before excusing me, he actually insisted I roll up my shirt sleeves to prove I didn't have *Etta* tattooed to one of my forearms. We've got to come out with a powerful retraction about changing the town name," Mr. Harold said, bobbing to his desk. "Flux, flux, flux," he muttered after setting down and picking up a pencil. "I never should have gone along with it. Every which way you look: Flux, flux, flux."

Maybe Gaylord would get straightened out by Benjamin Bortz and go to work for a new boss named Mr. Hugo Something, Henryetta couldn't help hoping, but she swallowed her tongue. Mr. Harold was already unmoderated enough, without being told he might have to write another powerful retraction of the editorial he'd gone ahead and put out —contrary to her modified advice—about harmful side effects of a Gaylord statue being put up in town.

THIRTY

Jonathan sat at his regular corner table at the Chair Crushers Cafe, looking through a fly-specked window, not liking what he saw. On the Kellogg's Korner parcel across a road from him—now fenced with chicken wire—Mexican criminals, no doubt those who had moved into the mobile houses set along the property frontage, were out in the plowed field that Merlene's no- account boy, Bart, intended to make into a so-called organic vegetable farm and vineyard. They were digging and raking and hauling stuff here and there like a swarm of industrious ants. In addition, garage doors at the back of the dilapidated service station building were open, auto repairs appeared to be in progress. Fortunately, the boxy houses were mobile. Soon as he got title to the property from the town, he would have his ranch hands come down some night and tow them up to his farmland north of town. Chances were the Mexicans would wake up the next morning, not knowing they had been relocated, and set themselves to tilling his ground. SWOPs tended to be hard workers, he'd noticed, but soon as they finished with his chores, at government expense, they would have to go.

The illegal home invasion problem, as Jonathan now saw it, was that Bailey's fence across the Interstate had not been big and strong enough. And under the Mayor's unenergetic leadership, law enforcement had been piss-poor. Jonathan considered himself very energetic, and smart, very, very smart. Having attended military school, if he himself were Mayor, a solid brick wall, forty feet high, would still be standing. Detentions would not have been so friendly. Forced turn-arounds of illegals would have been made with bayonets at the ready. But—thanks only to his private efforts—more of this local "Sanctuary City" bullroar would peter out soon enough, he thought. To grease the skids, he himself, on his own dime, had printed and circulated flyers, urging would-be Mexican rapers, in Spanish, to continue east on the interstate a few miles, to where they were guaranteed to win *un millon pesos* at the Creek Nation Casino.

Already there were signs of more outflux than influx of illegals. Bunkhouse food now went mostly uneaten, though local fast food joints had rolled up the welcome mats. Even Jorge, the semi-Mexican proprietor of the Chair Crushers Cafe, had found religion. A sign out front now said *English Language Menu Only,* in Spanish. Inside the front door—gifted to Jorge, gratis, from Jonathan's private collection—a life-size Miss Ann bobble-head doll now greeted trespassers. A tall, always-lit candle stood on the floor between her legs. An arched overhead sign warned, in Spanish: *Santa Ann Eats Mexican Children for Dessert.*

And speaking of Miss Ann, so to speak, Jonathan looked at his watch. In only about two more hours, CNN was to launch a new version of its old *Crossfire* show—re-branded *AMBUSH!*— pitting a guy named Jon Stewart against various guests in front of live college campus audiences. Promos he'd read described Stewart as a comedian, whose TV newsman schtick had led an entire youthful generation to rely on his Comedy Channel performances for real misinformation. Reportedly, the funny fellow and his act had got tiresome, but now somewhat older fans had demanded his return to TV, and an equally desperate CNN—no longer in the news business—had booked him to cater to a new young market of college students thirsting for political guidance. Tonight Stewart was scheduled to take on the long, lean cougar, and Jonathan could hardly wait to see Miss Ann bare her claws.

To kill time back at the Bunkhouse penthouse after supper, he set himself to curry-combing the slightly mangy white coat of his live-in horse, Polly. Years ago, out at the ranch, one of his ex-wives, the one also named Polly, had objected to him bringing another *JAH*-branded female inside the house, he recalled. Hell, he put his initials on the rumps of all the stock he owned, there was nothing romantic between him and Polly — the horse — but Polly — the wife — put her back foot down. There wasn't room for two Pollys in the house, she said, so… Jonathan found another comb for grooming the now stuffed Polly's mane. For his later move from the ranch into town, to fit Polly into the penthouse elevator, he'd had to saw-off her legs at the hocks. But with her hooves stuck back on, she — the horse — looked pretty as ever and was now about as easy to mount as the other… Noticing that it was now seven, Jonathan climbed onto Polly, clicked on a wall-mounted TV, and… There she was: Miss Ann, standing across from a serious-faced fella: that comedian, Stewart, no doubt.

"Welcome to *CAM-PUUUUS AM-BUUUUSH*, here in the Eleanor Roosevelt Martial Arts Arena of Harvard University!" said a youngish-looking, gray-haired little guy standing between them.

Rah, rah, rah…

"Are you locked and loaded, ladies?" he asked the crowd of mostly college girls.

Rah, rah, rah…

"Okay, fire away!"

"Jon, your totally dumb opponent says Republicans should

be allowed to freely engage in speech against unarmed students on clearly marked violence-free campuses because we make easy targets. Say something wickedly smart about that."

Stewart leaned into the camera, made a face and said, "F********k."

Ha, ha, ha, ha, ha, ha, ha, ha, ha, ha, ha, ha, ha, ha, ha, ha, ha, ha...

The camera switched to Miss Ann. "As I have often observed, liberals have no interest—or aptitude—for persuasion," she answered in that stuck-up boarding school drawl of hers. "If liberals were prevented from ever again calling conservatives dumb, they would be robbed of half their arguments. To be sure, they would still have 'racist', 'fascist', 'homophobe,' 'ugly,' and a few other highly nuanced arguments in the quiver, such as 'f**k'. But the loss of 'dumb' would cripple them."

"Racist!"

"Fascist!

"Homophobe!"

"You're ugly!" someone had the nerve to yell.

"And dumb!" shouted another Harvard woman.

"F*****k," Stewart repeated.

Ha, ha, ha, ha, ha, ha, ha, ha, ha, ha, ha, ha, ha, ha, ha, ha, ha...

"Okay, 'Miss' Coulter', since you supposedly are a woman, will you support our feminist cause and help us make a President out of Hillary Clinton? Duh, how about it, 'Miss' Coulter, <u>are</u> you a woman?"

"Have you noticed that all the girly-power, so-called feminists prominently engaged in national political affairs got to where they are through marriages to powerful spouses?" Miss Ann shot back. "I refer not only to Hillary Clinton, but also to Nancy

Pelosi, Arianna Huffington, and of course, John Kerry."

Boo, boo, boo...

"What the F**k," Stewart said, making an even unfunnier, smirky face.

Ha, ha, ha, ha...

SMACK! An egg splattered against Miss Ann's forehead, but she didn't even flinch.

Ha, ha, ha, ha, ha, ha, ha, ha, ha, ha, ha, ha, ha, ha...

Even the moderator thought the assault was hilarious. Jonathan was incensed.

"Hopefully, that's the last one you ever lay," Miss Ann calmly said in response to the egg attack. "Infertility of young liberal women may be civilization's last hope for survival, which is why I favor government sponsored sterilization throughout academia. And it's your loss. If you, my dear, miraculously ever got 'lucky' and carried a fertilized ova into a third trimester, Planned Parenthood would have bought the little 'it' from you, at a 'healthy', albeit wholesale price."

Boo, boo, boo...

"Now hold on there, Miss Coulter," said the girly, gray-haired moderator. "This is *AMBUSH*, not *Crossfire*. Jon, please, say something cleverly funny about a woman's choice to throw away or sell."

"F**k."

Ha, ha, ha, ha, ha, ha, ha, ha, ha, ha, ha, ha, ha, ha...

"So I guess there would be no point asking you, 'Miss' Coulter, if you support our petition to change the name of Harvard to Hillary University. The old, white male founder, John Harvard, was a dirty capitalist, you know. The money he gave to start this university was made off the backs of low-wage labor."

Rah, rah, rah...

"Why not? 'Ms.' Clinton is a proven liar of historical proportions. She would be an apt namesake and perfect model for the left-wing fascist propaganda machine this university has become, though of course you really should then wash your hands of all that dirty capital and turn out the lights on your way out."

Boo, boo, boo...

"I am much more concerned," said Miss Ann, "about the cuckoo idea hatched by one of your fellow so-called feminists—running for Mayorette—to alter the name of a heartland town that has been in the news lately: Henryetta, Oklahoma. By lopping off 'Henry', if elected, she would effectively divorce its long gone namesakes, Henry and Etta Beard."

Jonathan's ears perked up, along with his blood pressure, as Miss Ann went on talking about <u>his</u> own town:

"The editor of the local paper, who must be a fairly recent graduate of Harvard, has the equally nonsensical gall to favor the change on grounds related to protecting traditional marriage. But the Christian Bible is quite clear on the subject of posthumous divorce: 'Married couples whom a Justice of the Peace has buried six feet under, let no Mayoral candidate dig up and put asunder'."

Boo, boo, boo...

"C'mon, Stewart. Wake up and say something brilliantly funny."

Jonathan clicked off the TV sound. He was sorry to leave Miss Ann standing there alone, proud and straight as a fence post covered in bird droppings—"flipping the bird" back at Harvard—but now he had even more important matters on his mind. Damnit! Naturally, he had always taken it for granted that the town was named for his great grandfather, Hugh Henry, who had settled the territory it set on. And without thinking much about it, he had figured the tacked-on "etta," might have been an Indian or Irish term for, say, "small town." Now that he did think about it, Jonathan could imagine that "Etta" could have been the name of Grandpa Hugh's horse, but no, not a wife. Hell, Grandpa Hugh, part Creek Indian and part Irish, owned the damned town and conveyed a land title to part of his holdings only after local squatters got him drunk one day. Not one to waste time on local politics, or reading the local newspaper, Jonathan had not known there was talk of changing the town name to... what? "Etta," for a woman?!

Jonathan dismounted, went to a gun rack and checked to make sure his trusty two-barrel shotgun was fully loaded. Damnit, he'd had enough of that sissy-Mayor, Bailey, and more than enough bullroar out of that not so little beaver, Hilde-lard Bottomly. He put the shotgun up to his shoulder, aiming to see to it that his hometown was rightly re-named plain Henry—as in Hugh, and Jonathan Henry --- Oklahoma.

I WAS NAMED FOR SIR EDMUND HILLARY, FAMOUS CONQUEROR OF MOUNT EVEREST.

*Hillary Clinton, born 1947, when Sir Edmund
was an unknown beekeeper*

THIRTY ONE

Henryetta woke up to the screeching sound of a siren signaling a town emergency. Outside her Shangri-La singles-only apartment, after seeing no signs of stormy weather in the pre-dawn sky, nor red glare of a big fire on a horizon, she ran to her Checker and headed lickety-split for downtown. Slowed down and cruising on Main Street in dim light, she noticed nothing out of the ordinary. Passing by the Bunkhouse Motel...

Halt! someone hollered through a bullhorn. She halted. **Get out of the vehicle with your hands up!** She got out of the Checker and raised her arms, wondering what in tarnation... **For cryin' out loud, Henryetta, do you <u>want</u> to get raped by a Mexican?** It was Mayor Bailey, she saw, crouching in a half-opened doorway to the motel. **Get in here and cover yourself,** he ordered.

Inside the motel lobby, a jail clerk, Ms. Wheeler, handed her a prisoner's orange jumpsuit to wear over her nightie. The Mayor went back to peeking out to the street. The town's police force—all three of them, not including Chief Potter—squatted at a window, pointing their guns through the plate glass. What in tarnation was goin' on?

"Jail break by Mexican rapers with criminal records," Mayor

Bailey whispered over his shoulder. "They got loose and started tearing up the whole dern town. Remain calm. I've called in the National Guard."

Also in a whisper, Ms. Wheeler explained: "A G-man: Big, ugly, semi-redheaded fella came in at midnight. Stuck out his big barrel-chest and ordered me to turn over all the remaining Mexicans to him. But he had no deputies, no manacles, not even a gun, and soon as they got out the door, well, the Mexicans went wild and started runnin' up and down Main Street, huntin' for blonde women, no doubt. With Chief Potter on vacation, I had no choice except call Mayor Bailey."

Henryetta scooted back over to the door and peered past the crouching Mayor. "Just look at all the damage they've done," he said. "What we have on our hands is a full-scale hometown invasion." With the sun coming up, she saw... Oh yeah, a few store windows had been smashed, some signs stuck onto storefronts were in tatters, but ... Land sakes alive! The only signs still in place were Ms. Bottomly's *I Am Woman!* posters. All the *Mayor* thumbs signs had been tore down! No doubt the Mexicans were mad at Mayor Bailey for pullin' them off the Interstate and puttin' them in the Bunkhouse Motel, she reckoned. Maybe local folks really were in danger. Worried about her mother, Henryetta climbed over the Mayor. Wynona Sue had turned her hair from burnt auburn back to blonde recently, and... Just as she got to her Checker, uh oh, here they came again, a whole bunch of Mexicans, hootin' and hollerin' somethin' fierce, on horseback!

"**Hallelujah!**" the Mayor hollered from behind her. "The National Guard boys, and just in the nick of time!"

Henryetta was relieved, but then the mounted National Guard troops, none in army uniforms, commenced to—of all things—rip down Ms. Bottomly's signs!

"**Hurrah!**" the Mayor shouted, running toward them, but... Out of nowhere, a gray blur shot past Henryetta and—land sakes alive—knocked poor ol' Mayor Bailey to the ground! A bullhorn and a gray wig flew into the air and... Land sakes alive again, it was Aunt Maude—semi-redheaded without her wig on—who went to pounding the Mayor with her fists, cussing him like a mad housewife who'd caught a no-account husband sneakin' into the house at sunrise with Friendly Creature on his breath and lipstick on his shirt. It took the town's entire police force, except for Chief Potter, to finally get Ms. Bottomly's friend off him.

"Arrest the son of a bitch!" the usually kindly-seeming head of the Homes Sweet Homes Association shouted, as they dragged her into the Bunkhouse Motel. "That bastard, Bailey, is guilty of dirty politics!"

Henryetta was re-relieved. The entire fracas—also likely including Aunt Maude's off the record accusation that the Mayor had tried to sex assault her—amounted to nothing more than dirty tricks played by politicians on both sides of the Mayoral election, she reckoned. But it was news, and her job was to put it in the paper.

After letting herself into the *Weekly Herald* storefront office, Henryetta set down at her desk and fired up her computer. Before starting to word process a report, she checked her mailbox and... *Henryetta - My phone is dead and wi-fi- is in and out. With desperate hope that you get this, I have attached my notes for your use, in case something happens to me. God willing, I will be out of harm's way and in Dallas with Gaylord prior to his scheduled "conformation" at high noon tomorrow. Pray for me. Ben.*

Gaylord's "conformation"? Harm's way? Pray for me? In a

sweat, Henryetta stripped off the orange prisoner outfit. Worried sick about the message Benjamin had sent last night, she opened an attached file labeled *Gaylord and Me*:

Driving from Gaylord's hometown of Henryetta, Oklahoma into the heavily wooded southeastern part of the state known as Little Dixie, Gaylie confided to me that the family of his Dallas Cowboys teammate, Billy Ray Williams, lived on a secluded farm with other members of a Nacirema Church of the Holy Cow. I thought, and hoped, he might be jesting, but after getting off a paved highway and traveling at least twenty miles on dirt roads, we came upon a hanging, life-size, tin silhouette of a cow, enigmatically "branded" with pink paint as "LORNA 42D-30-36." Gaylord said he was not at liberty to tell what the name and numbers meant. Inside flanking sections of barbed wire fence, driving on a rutted, barely passable farm wagon path, I saw no actual cows, but only several large women in long gray dresses who, Gaylord said, were "grazing" on huckleberries. Well into the farm, I then saw five or six dairy barns surrounded by chicken wire fencing, but still no cows. Gaylord identified a large nearby building, its double-domed roof painted pink, as the "brasserie" where The Mister—Nacirema Church leader and Billy Ray's father—performed "cleavage ceremonies."

Cleavage ceremonies? Henryetta became more alarmed about what Gaylord had got hisself into. Right after Benjamin's prior mention of Gaylord's planned "conformation" or "confirmation," she had looked up the terms. One meant to go through a baptism ritual to be be admitted as a full member of a church. But the other meant to comply with certain standards, possibly by getting "adjusted" to a similar form or type! Picturing Gaylie on the cover of *US Weekly* magazine, with long hair extensions, Henryetta went back to reading:

Inside a kind of vestibule, dimly illuminated only by candles, we were warmly greeted by three large-bosomed women, all middle-aged, all in long gray dresses, all with hair pulled back into buns and all —collectively—introduced by Gaylord as Billy Ray's "mama." One of them, who happened to have a noticeable dark mustache, politely explained that since I was not yet officially under consideration for conformation, I would not be allowed to accompany them into an inner sanctum to meet The Mister, which proved to be fortuitous. For after they left me alone, I noticed a pink cloth spread on a table between two candlesticks next to duplicate autographed black-and-white photos of Dolly Parton. Embroidered on the cloth with golden thread were the words "Nacirema Magical Beliefs and Body Rituals." Beneath the cloth, I found a worn and weathered book, untitled but attributed to "Horace Miner, Prophet of the Nacirema People." I took a deep breath and opened the book.

Following is approximately what the Gospel of Horace tells:

To the Nacirema believer, the human body is ugly, and its natural tendency is to debility and disease. Incarcerated in such a body, mankind's only hope is to avert these influences through powerful use of ritual and ceremony, for which purpose every household must have one or more shrines… walled in stone… adorned with pottery plaques… focal point of which is a built-in box or chest for the keeping of many charms and magical potions for preservation of worshipers. Beneath each charm box is a small font. Each day, every member of a Nacirema family, in succession, is required to enter the shrine, bow his head, mingle different sorts of holy water in the font, and proceed with a brief ablution.

At that point in my furtive reading of the Horace Gospel, though appalled by description of a ritualistic practice of inserting hog hairs and magical powder into the mouths of church members, I admit, I was intrigued. Despite strange gurgling noises coming from the brasserie's inner sanctum, I read deeper into the mystery of a chamber called the "latipso," where female supplicants are stripped of their clothes in preparation of rites used to make their breasts larger. Women achieving hypermammary development are apparently so idolized by Nacirema believers they are able to charge fees simply for permission to stare at them.

Henryetta looked up from reading Benjamin's notes and silently said a little prayer that he would be able to get Gaylord out of the harmful ways of what sounded to her like one of those strange religious cults she'd heard about. Having never known his own mama—or had a big-breasted girlfriend that she knew of—Gaylord would likely be a sucker for Billy Ray's "collective" top-heavy bunch. On the other hand, Billy Ray hisself was not only a male, but a particularly skinny one, at that. She couldn't help wondering what Gaylord would see in him. Dreading the worst, Henryetta returned to Benjamin's notes:

Before I could find out more about Nacirema rituals, however, the door from the inner sanctum creaked open behind me. I turned, and there stood a large barrel-chested person wearing—of all things—a stunning Beau Brummell dressing gown, who I initially mistook for Billy Ray's mustachioed mama, holding in a gloved hand what I mistook for a ping-pong paddle. Only later did I learn that I had been caught reading the holy Book of Horace by none other than The Mister himself, and that the ceremonial object he held was a sacred cleavager.

Oh no, not a cleavager! Henryetta rose up halfway out of her chair before realizing that even if she jumped in her Checker and took off lickety-split into Little Dixie, she would have no more chance than a blind pig looking for a skillet in a dark clothes closet of ever finding the Nacirema Church of the Holy Cow by high noon. Gaylord was caught in the gloved hand of The Mister, with no one to help him out of the fix except Benjamin Bortz. Dang that no-account Billy Ray Williams!

THIRTY TWO

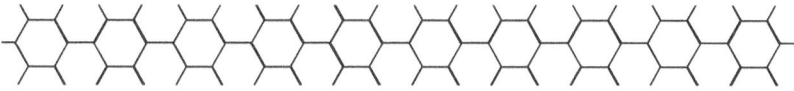

Inside her Division Street house, behind closed window shades and locked doors, Hilde ended an especially annoying call from the HSH lawyer in Washington. On the other hand, she then realized that under the circumstances, for a pesky Republican Congressman to heartlessly pick, pick, pick at her innocent marital relationship with Buddy and alleged association with the Homes Sweet Homes Foundation, signified that she, like Virgil Carter four years ago, had been recognized as a rising star in the Democratic Party. At this stage, a retroactive divorce was not a viable option for building a firewall between her and her ne'er do good husband. More clear-cut severance of their connection was needed, and fast. But in addition to completely dropping her married name, what more could she do? Hilde sighed. Once upon a time, her partner in life had been supportive. Exchanging vows in front of a Justice of the Peace, Buddy Moon had solemnly promised that the other cheap floozy in attendance — her so-called maid of honor — meant nothing to him. And more importantly, that after he had achieved fame and fortune, it would be her turn in the limelight, but... Now, yet again, he had let her down.

Pacing the living room floor, she glanced at her watch, then clicked on a television. She should be rehearsing spontaneity for an unavoidable upcoming public debate against Bailey that Maude had agreed to on her own. Not that she was the slightest bit concerned about going toe-to-toe with the bumbling boob. In rebuttal to her one-two punch—"I Am Woman, but also Manly"—what could he say? That he was "Man," but also effeminate? That was not how the modern-day double standard worked. No, she wasn't the slightest bit worried about the debate, and Hillary Clinton was scheduled to be interviewed by Joe and Mika on *Morning Joe*, which was timely. No one could bob-and-weave her way out of a corner with skill equal to Hillary. Her TV appearance today might deliver some needed tips, but...

To Hilde's chagrin, her rival—in a peach, not bright orange outfit, and with both eyes true blue—appeared on the screen, looking fabulously botoxed to the hilt. Her finger-waving to persons in the audience went on for several minutes, pleasant chit-chat with her hosts for endless minutes longer. Finally: "Mrs. Clinton, with regard to the subpoena issued to you last week," Morning Joe asked, "will you cooperate with the FBI or resist the efforts of law enforcement authorities to examine your dirty laundry?"

Hillary, bright eyed and beaming, seemed both surprised and delighted to have just then heard the news that she too was under investigation.

"The G-men are trying to verify or disprove your account of how you reacted to the Benghazi bulletin," Mika helpfully explained, "by checking your panties for stains and interrogating Mrs. Weiner, who reportedly washes your unmentionables."

Hillary straightened her back. "I'm afraid I will have to disappoint my political opponents this time," she replied, still beaming. "You know, Mika, another cross-dresser, J. Edgar, played this same dirty trick when Eleanor Roosevelt was running the Oval Office, for the same kinky purpose. And so did you, Joe," she added, not beaming, "when you pretended to be impeaching my husband for what he did, totally by accident, to that blue dress. I now routinely burn my underwear immediately after usage."

"Let's move on to cleaner politics," Joe suggested. "Mrs. Clinton, what is your response to opponents and other critics who say your flip-flopping on important issues makes the Bruce-to-Caitlyn change of position look like small potatoes by comparison?"

Hillary swiveled to look directly, and earnestly, into the camera. "As a woman who has also been trapped in a man's, uh, world, I empathize deeply with Caitlyn's prior victimhood. As a woman, I applaud Caitlyn's brave defense of all women's inalienable right to change their mind. As a woman myself, as well as a mother and grandmother, I say to Caitlyn, and all male-to-female transgender voters, that in the comfortable surroundings of the 'ladies room', so to speak, you are welcome to flip-flop as much as you desire."

"Are you now endorsing only a transgender woman's right to pee, or... "

Sounds of fumbling with the back door lock were followed by the rattle of crockery in the kitchen, then Maude's wigless appearance. "Sit down and brace yourself, Hilde,' said her obviously frazzled campaign manager, after staggering into the living room with a cup of coffee in hand. "The shit has hit the fan." Seated across from her, Maude reported that the ungrateful residents of the HSH Hogback Haciendas had refused to accept any walking-around money and seemed uninterested in taking part in the American democratic process. "For some strange reason, they are content to work for a living on that damned organic vegetable farm out there, and don't even want the right to vote for you in the upcoming election. They will pay for their disloyalty," her local HMS franchisee said, before also reporting that she had been forced to spring the Mexican detainees with criminal records from the Bunkhouse Motel jail annex. "But brace yourself, Hilde," she said again, after gulping down more coffee. "The freed Hilde's Helpers completed their assigned task, but right after I paid them off and sent them on down the road, Mayor Thumbs came to his own rescue."

"You were seen? Maude, I will have to deny ever knowing you."

Maude emptied her mug and wiped her mouth with the back of a hand. "I hid behind a lamp post," she said, "but... Brace yourself, Hilde. A gang of rowdies rode into downtown on horseback and—brace yourself—they tore down all of your signs!"

Hilde, outraged by her opponent's dirty political tactics, leapt to her feet to confront her inept so-called Helper. "And you were not armed, were you. You just cowered behind a lamp post and let them... I want Bailey charged with felonious campaigning!"

"I did charge him, Hilde. The son of a bitch will have to debate with casts on both broken thumbs, and two black eyes."

"A good first step, Maude, but he has to pay the ultimate price for his crime."

"He pled 'Uncle', Hilde, and promised to pay for new signs, but..."

"That's not enough, not by a long shot. I want Bailey eliminated from the race. I demand that I be elected without having to go through this meaningless debate you got me into without my permission."

"Hilde, brace yourself," her dim-witted advisor said yet again. Hilde sat down and — as Maude seemed to search for words — began to aimlessly pick at a black lace border sewn onto a pillow, fretting about the "Buddy" problem. "Hilde, I... I... I hate to to bear bad tidings, but... " Maude stammered, "Jonathan Henry has... Now the only name on any downtown building is his own." So what, that was nothing new. "The Jonathan" obviously had a fetish about applying his *JAH* brand to everything he touched, including her derriere, though in that case — thanks to magic-marker ink depletion — he'd failed to get past *J*. "No, Hilde, it's a political problem," Maude said. "The cavalry that rode down Main Street, they... they were not Buford Bailey's horsemen, after all. They were cowboys from the JAH Ranch, no doubt ordered to sabotage your campaign by none other than The Jonathan himself!"

Though surprised by the news, Hilde was hardly shocked. Men were not to be trusted, they said one thing, did another, and somehow got away with it. No doubt Jonathan Henry was in a typically adolescent boyish pet for having not gotten a second helping of tuna casserole served to him. Oh well, another soak in his penthouse hot tub would be among the lesser humiliations she'd endured to achieve her ambitions, but... Damnit, if only she had been born with a penis!

"... in a peevish pet," Maude confirmed. "Apparently Jonathan just now heard about your bold initiative to change the town name to 'Etta', and... Hilde, he has entered the War on Women against you. He's posted his own black-and-white signs in favor of *HENRY!* on virtually every Main Street building, even onto the backs of numerous local citizens!"

As Maude paused to fan herself and catch her breath, Hilde fussed with the black lace border she had picked loose from the sofa pillow.

"Don't you see, Hilde," said Maude, twisting a hankie in her hands. "Jonathan Henry is running for Mayor! He will be in tomorrow night's debate, on national television!"

As Maude went on to wail about Jonathan Henry having name recognition, unlimited resources, and no doubt leverage over countless town voters, Hilde semi-aimlessly put the black lace—a *mantilla* of sorts—upon her head, which brought her friend's defeatist talk to a sudden end. "My Goddess, Hilde," she said, with a worried expression on her wrinkled homely face, "it's not the end of the world. You look like you're in… in mourning."

"Well, so be it," Hilde said, getting up from the sofa. "Buddy hasn't been heard from in weeks, but his shoes and some of his clothes have been found, washed up on a beach in Mexico," she said, looking at herself in a wall mounted mirror. "Over-exerting himself in the arms and between the legs of some bimbo, he may well have fallen off the deck of a yacht—or even a cheap floating air mattress—and left me to fend for myself."

Maude came to her side, put a consoling arm around her shoulder, and also looked into the mirror. "Brilliant!" said her campaign manager. "Hilde Bottomly: Wronged woman and grieving widow. Absolutely brilliant!"

THIRTY
THREE

Henryetta looked up at a clock mounted to a wall in the *Weekly Herald* office. Dang! Only seven minutes had passed since she'd last checked the time, while more than thirty-six hours had gone by since Benjamin sent the message about Gaylord from a farm somewhere down in Little Dixie. And she'd had no answer to her calls and e-mails to him. Was Benjamin able to rescue Gaylord from The Mister's cleavager before any conformation by the Holy Cow Church took place? Were Gaylord and him in Dallas by now, out of harm's way of the Nacirema cult headed up by Billy Ray's daddy and collective mamas? She was rarin' at the bit to head on down that way and search for as long as it took to find out what happened, or didn't happen, but... Dang it, the Mayoral election was only two days away and Mr. Harold had come unspooled. No doubt due to pressures of the culture wars that had broke out in town, her boss had run off to a brain spa out in Arizona for nerve attack treatments. So for now and the foreseeable future, she her own self was in charge of putting out the paper.

It was mostly her own fault, Henryetta had to admit. She felt dreadful sorry to have stirred up Mr. Harold with that wisecrack about Gaylord getting married in a dress. And to have egged him on to take a stand from where he set on the issue of changing the town name to plain ol' Etta, which had got him called into the high school principal's office, no doubt for the first time in his whole life. Even worse, someone on cable news had got wind of his editorial, and said on national TV that by "disrespecting the ties that bound Henry and Etta Beard," a married couple, he had undermined the whole idea of traditional marriage between man and woman, which was the exact opposite of the powerful point he'd intended to make. Then, late yesterday...

Henryetta looked up from her work to see, not the wall clock, but the frowning face of a stout, very short-haired woman—chewing on an unlit cigar—standing there with hands on a set of ample hips. "Where's that sumbitch, Harold Mixon?" she said in a gruff voice. "And how big an ol' boy is he, anyway? Not that it matters half as much as a mouse fart in a wind storm to yours truly, Sharon Gene-by-God Mercer. He hung up on me yesterday, so I've come down early from Tulsa to personally deliver a forty-gallon drum of whup-ass to the sumbitch."

Henryetta explained that Mr. Harold was out of town for an extended mental rest in Arizona.

"Sumbitch!" said the woman, tossing her cigar butt in the general direction of a trash can. "Tomorrow night's debate was late gettin' put together, and I was countin' on Mixon to come up with local skinny for the media panel."

Debate? Henryetta hadn't heard nothing about no debate.

The manlyish woman explained that she was an organizer for Local 63 of the Tulsa Chapter of the League of Women Voters, and had a deal with the Public Broadcasting TV System to sponsor a nationally televised debate between the three local Mayoral candidates. "Your small-town local fight has got widespread public attention, as a kind of undercard of next year's heavyweight Presidential bout," she said, "almost just like four years ago when that sumbitch, Carter, ran for County Commissioner. I've got Judy Woodruff and Rachel Maddow lined up to take down the two male palookas in the ring, but... Damnit, I need a local moderator to point out their weak spots." Now Henryetta semi-understood why Mr. Harold had run out of the office in a hysterical fit, after putting down his phone and hollering that "goons" were putting "the muscle" on him.

In answer to Ms. Mercer asking, she told that she her own self was the *Weekly Herald's* only reporter, and had been covering the Mayoral election. In answer to the League of Women Voters organizer's next gruff question, she said, yes, she her own self was a female and had a better set of clothes at her singles-only Shangri-La apartment. But as for taking Mr. Harold's place as moderator—which ordinarily would have made her excited as all get out—Henryetta felt obliged to admit that she had took Ms. Bottomly's side in the election, and in fact had several *I Am Woman!* signs stuck on her yellow Checker.

"No problem," Ms. Mercer said. "Just don't make it too obvious. With a little steering on your part, the bigtime TV anchor babes will be on those two ol' country boys like red ants on a spilt snow cone. It ain't notin' for either one of 'em to whup a man's ass. Be at the high school gym tomorrow evening at six, to bring Judy and Rachel up to speed."

Left alone, even more excited than all get out about being on a nationally televised debate panel with Judy Woodruff and another goon named Rachel Something—as moderator, no less—Henryetta looked up to the wall clock. Surprised at how fast time had flown, she decided to get back to worrying about Gaylord after the big debate.

THIRTY
FOUR

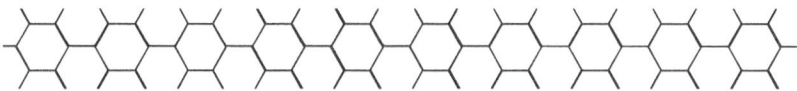

Satisfied that outside agitators had moved on— including in particular the ones who wanted to "shoot the Sheriff"—Buford ventured onto the Main Street sidewalk, only to find a still hostile political environment. Almost every male citizen he encountered wore a black-and-white sticker on his chest in favor of *HENRY.* Dang near every single one of the women had on a pink pin in support of the even more radical movement for *ETTA.* He was caught in the middle, of nowhere, still with no settled strategy for playing the contentious name game. And while his two opponents had used their catchy positions to get attention to other things that aimed to widen their appeal, the center—where he was forced to stay put as Mayor of all the people—had gotten cramped from both sides, and was getting narrow as a bargain basement coffin.

Plus, he now had two black eyes that made him look like a masked bank robber, and plaster casts on both thumbs that undoubtedly made him also seem too physically handicapped to steer the town in any direction.

Dang it, that... that Bottomly woman had about cornered the female vote, he imagined, based on nothing but her gender. And now she was putting out flyers and spreading rumors that made her look also manlier than Arnold Schwarzenegger in his buffed, and greased-up prime. Under her administration, she claimed the high school football team would be feared by all comers, because it would again be called the "Fighting Hens." Female chickens, though protective of younguns, were strict about maintaining law and order, one of her flyers said, which was where the term "pecking order" for keeping people in line came from. Chickens were empathetic team players, she said, but were not to be trifled with, which was why the saying "mad as a wet hen" originated in the Bible. And supposedly barnyard fowl like her were meat eaters that feasted on other creatures such as mice and lizards.

Earlier today, she had come out of hiding to stand in a makeshift chicken wire pen set up by the town's World War I Doughboy statue, and shout: "Poultry are the closest surviving relatives of Tyrannosaurus-Rex, and just as scary. The Fighting Hens of Etta, Oklahoma—led by me as your Mayor—will beat the living shit out of every bunch of Redskins, Blue Demons, White Supremacists, Ruf-Neks, Mighty Mice and Fighting Lizards that dare to take the field against us!" Dang it, Bottomly was running on a sign platform of *I Am Woman!* but also trying to have a cake and eat it like a macho man!

Having never been on any athletic team, or debate squad, Buford had no clue about how to counter-punch, even if he'd had the stomach—and clinchable fists—to hit a woman.

Hemming him in from the other side, Mr. Henry had softened his public image to not look so much like a macho man: By promising mobile homes on his farmland north of town to poor Mexicans at half the price charged by Bottomly's buddy, Rouser, at the Hogback Haciendas. And by posting different family pictures on his *Henry* signs all over town, showing him sitting by a fireplace, or grilling a chicken on a patio, or relaxing in a hot tub with one or another of <u>six</u> different bosomy wives and lots of children gathered 'round him.

Having never been married and sired kids, Buford didn't have any such warm-and-fuzzy photos to show, and his mother refused to pose for one with him unless her entire canine family was included, which would have made it look like he was the town's incumbent Dog Catcher.

On the other hand, inside his think tank earlier, Buford had begun to think: Local voters, ignorant and unengaged about important political things, really didn't give a rat's a-s-s about all the issues that cable television news had put up in the air. Or even if they did care, they knew in their hearts and minds that no politician—from Mayor to Governor to President—would or could do anything about what riled them, including even pot holes. So for the big televised debate with his opponents coming up tonight, only hours before tomorrow's Election Day, for him to continue his career in public service, not to mention rise to even higher office, Buford decided he had to focus on the related hot button issues of town name and mascot.

Fortunately, he found a ready-made, fully-manned focus group assembled at Moe & Curly's barber shop, though unfortunately, *Henry* signs were plastered not only on the shop storefront—controlled by Mr. Henry— but also on its interior walls. "You're welcome to wait your turn for a trim around the edges, Booster," Moe said. "But no speeches. Everyone's mind is made up about two things: The Jonathan knows how to run a bidness, and you are a bullshitter." *Ha, ha has*, came from the whole group. "I know, I know," Buford answered, "but hear me out." *Ha, ha, ha...* "What if, I'm just sayin', what if we made peace here in town by re-naming... " With Moe and Curly facing him from behind their barber chairs, two customers in the chairs looking at him, and four others just hanging out, he floated a first trial balloon:

"What would you say about just starting over and... I'm just spit-balling, but... What if we re-named the town, oh, say, maybe Springfield?"

"Doh," said Moe, who only semi-resembled one of the Three Stooges, "we already have a Springfield, and... "

"Springfield already has a Mayor, and that fella Quimby is doin' a good enough job, I'd say," Curly opined, "tending to pot holes, like Mayors are s'posed to do."

"Yeah, Buford, if we voted for 'Springfield' and kept you on the job," someone said, "do you reckon we might get a few pot holes fixed?"

"Might as well just officially name this town 'Pot Hole'," someone else said. "There's plenty of towns called Springfields around the country. Another one here might confuse the post office about getting my government check to me on time."

"Say, by golly, you're right about that, Vern," said Curly. "I say just let sleeping dogs lay on the porch, along with 'Lazy-Boy' Bailey." *Ha, ha, ha, ha, ha, ha...*

"Okay, okay, good point," Buford conceded, "but sleeping dogs sometimes just lay there, farting, and miss all the trucks that go by. About everything is in flux these days. The town's gotta keep up with it."

"Farts cause flux?"

Buford sensed weakening commitment to the name *HENRY* and blew up another balloon. "How would you feel about an unextreme compromise that would satisfy everyone?" he asked. "What if... I'm just sayin'... What if we capitalized 'Etta', put a hyphen after 'Henry', plus added a second hyphen and second

'Henry' for Mr. Jonathan's grandpa, to make it all come out to 'Henry-Etta-Henry'?!" That way both men voters and women..."

"That's a good one, Thumbs," Moe said. "We could fight, fight, fight as the Three Humped Camels."

Ha, ha, ha, ha, ha...

"Hyphen? What the hell is a 'hyphen'?"

"Don't be ignorant," said Curly. "Just imagine, in print on the sports page: **Henry-Etta-Henry Hyphens Punctuate the Lights Out of Seminole Semi-Colons**."

Ha, ha, ha, ha, ha, ha, ha, ha, ha...

"Okay, okay, very funny. Let's move on to what our real mascot might be," Buford suggested, "which is a related sub-issue my opponents are weak on. What would you think of the 'Fighting...'?"

"'Bullshitters' is what I think. Dang it, Buford, you promised to fix the damn pot holes, but you and every other dang reg'lar politician are plain ol' Bullshitters, with a capital B and no dang hyphenator. We need an unpolitician to come in and fix things."

Two hours later, in the Mayor's official office, Buford remained adrift from any ground whatever to stand on. Male voters would likely vote in droves for Mr. Henry, even though "The Jonathan" had not yet come up with a mascot to go with his name. And women, according to those in the focus group he'd later consulted at The Best Little Hair House beauty parlor, had also laughed out loud at his trial balloons. "Hymen? Between Henry and Etta Beard?" that Henryetta gal's sassy mama had said, cackling. "Too late, Booster, way too late." *Ha, ha, ha.* "Yeah, that cherry got plucked a long time ago," said another female hair styler. *Ha, ha, ha.* "Only a way out-of-date, way out-of-it bachelor man would think you could put that little thingy back in the bush," a third hair cutter-and-curler clucked. *Ha, ha, ha.* He'd left the beauty parlor, downright frightened about what would happen to the town if that... that Bottomly woman or any other female ever got elected.

Buford looked up to the pictures of his father and grandfather, Mayors Bailey the Number One and the Number Two, then hung his head in despair. With nothing to say, he thought he might as well drop out of the big debate. His chances of winning the election were thin as a slice of boarding house pie.

KNOCK! KNOCK!

"Who's there?"

"Hey, I got no time for dumb jokes," said a voice from the other side of the office door. "But I got a big load for personal delivery to a 'Mayor Buford P. Bailey' from a 'Dooley Doolittle' in Dallas, Texas, marked C.O.D. for shipping and handling charges."

Hallelujah! For the debate tonight, Buford had something concrete—or rather a subject in solid plaster—to shout about.

VII

DONALD TRUMP WAS HERE.
10/28/1957
Public Bathroom Wall/ Exxon Station/ Queens, New York

THIRTY FIVE

Entering the high school gym—already filled-up and bustling with fans of the three candidates—Henryetta felt semi-ashamed to have turned from being a proud Golden Knight into a Fighting Hen. Only a few years ago, she was a little ol' high school cheerleader, wanting to become a journalist and someday win one of those Pulitzer Prizes for telling good news stories. Now she felt like just the opposite, an ordinary small town newspaper reporter, rooting for Ms. Bottomly to win a big debate and get elected Mayor for the sake of changing the dern name of her little ol' hometown.

Hooters up for Henry! Henry! Henry! Hooters up...
Bottoms up for Bottomly! Bottomly! Bottomly! Bottoms up...

But her job was only to "steer" two famous television gals, who she had looked up on *Wikipedia*, and both seemed fair enough for news people, no matter what the League of Women Voters goon said. Ms. Woodruff had recently argued against her own friendly co-talker on PBS that she was <u>not</u> a member of a "liberal elite establishment." Though *Time* magazine reported "nice is the new nasty" in an article about Ms. Maddow from MSNBC, *The New Republic* magazine said she had "a perfectly settled perspective" that made the truth obvious to her without any questions getting asked.

We want Etta! We want Etta! We want Etta!

We want Henry! We want Henry! We want Henry!

And in the local skinny about Mayor Bailey that she had typed up for Ms. Woodruff and Ms. Maddow, Henryetta had drew the line against including any of the "Talking Points" listed on a sheet of paper someone had slid under the *Weekly Herald* back door last night. Whether or not the Mayor had an appetite for dog food was his own business, she reckoned. Rumor that Mayor Booster was "shacked up" with an illegal Mexican woman, and had "stood stud" for breeding anchor babies was too unbelievable to even make him deny it. Hopefully, the debate would focus on the name change issue and be polite as a church pie supper, but… Uh oh, up on the brightly lit debate stage, Ms. Sharon Gene-By-God Mercer from the League of Women Voters seemed to be telling who ate the cabbage to a blonde woman. The lanky gal was taller, younger and longer-haired than she'd pictured Ms. Woodruff. Henryetta went up the stage stairs to hear what was going on between them.

Fight! Fight! Fight for the Fighting Hens!

Fight! Fight! Fight against the Hens!

"… and you're not even a card carrying member of the League," Ms. Mercer was saying, with a face as puffed-up and red as Ms. Woodruff's was thin and white. "I saw you on *Ambush*, whuppin' Jon Stewart's ass like a borrowed mule. Dang it, I rented a Judy Woodruff, by God, and I'm not gonna settle for no Ann Coulter!"

"Judy had a fainting spell," said the blonde gal—apparently a Ms. Coulter—cool as a tall glass of lemonade. "The sight of ten Republican Presidential candidates on one debate stage last week must have been more than her delicate political condition could stand. When she heard your Ms. Bottomly was at risk of being gangbanged by two male opponents, well, she was already in shock that Big Bad Bernie had the balls to challenge Mrs. Clinton, one-on-one. So the speakers bureau sent me, based solely on gender, no doubt."

"It don't matter to me how big an' ol' gal you are," said Ms. Mercer,"looking up to the taller Ms. Coulter, with an unlit cigar clinched in her teeth. "I myself would never douse a woman with whup-ass, but if my little dog, Bon Jovi, happens to start humpin' your leg, you'd better have brung a lunch. Bon Jovi holds on tight as rust to a pump handle, and he's a biter."

Henry! Henry! Henry!
Etta! Etta! Etta!

Fortunately, Ms. Maddow showed up on the debate stage — her hair as dark brown and short as Ms. Coulter's extensions were blonde and long — with a bright-eyed look about her that reminded Henryetta of Benjamin Bortz. As the three of them went to jabbering, she had a little heart pang, worried that Gaylord might have got a Caitlyn treatment in the Holy Cow Church from Billy Ray's daddy, The Mister. Her typed-up skinny about all the foolish things "Thumbs" Bailey had said and done as Mayor didn't say nothing about that dern statue of Gaylie, and she aimed to steer the debate away from any mention of same-sex marriage that might bring up the plaster subject. In addition...

Henry! Henry! Henry!
Etta! Etta! Etta!
BUZZ!

Lights on the stage got brighter. One of Ms. Mercer's assistants turned on the gym scoreboard. "Okay, okay, showtime!" said the Women's Voter League organizer, pushing Henryetta toward and into the middle chair at a semi-long table, then leaning on her. "You are the official scorekeeper," Ms. Mercer croaked in her ear. "Don't let that right-wing bimbo so much as sprinkle a drop of whup-ass on Bottomly. Cut-off the two punch-drunk bums if either one so much as lays a glove on her. Final score oughta end up something like 99 to 1 to 1. Press the button to shut up too much… "

BUZZ!

THIRTY SIX

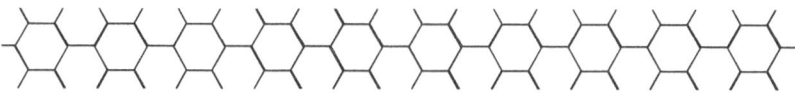

Standing beside a stage in the noisy high school gym, Hilde adjusted her black lace *mantilla.* Maude continued to babble at her side. In this very same arena, only weeks ago, she had boldly delivered a stirring manifesto against the ongoing Republican War on Women, little knowing at the time that her Fiftieth Reunion Address would so quickly become of historic importance to the entire nation. True, tonight's event was only a small town debate in connection with a stepping-stone local election, but virtually the entire local population had turned out to see and hear her. A vast television audience would also be watching. Power brokers in Washington and other large cities would be taking her measure for much higher office. So yes, Hilde was nervous, though Maude had assured her that Judy Woodruff from PBS and Rachel Maddow from MSNBC were BFF's, who would "tee it up" for her and "bust the balls" of her right-wing male opponents. Even so...

We want Henry! We want Henry! We want Henry!

"When you walk onto the stage, remember to be spontaneous, exactly the way we rehearsed," Maude said, yet again. "Smile, express delighted surprise to see your many friends in the audience, make little finger waves at them whether any are in attendance or not. Seek eye contact with Judy and Rachel. But do not wink, and no one will notice, uh, any absence of perfect eye-color coordination. Talk with an Okie accent, but don't overdo it. Just hyphenate every other syllable or so, and pronounce 'en' as 'in'. Be brave, let your mourning outfit say it all about your presumed tragic loss. If not asked about Buddy, wait for an appropriate time and another subject to let only a single teardrop run down your cheek. People like a victim, but not a cry baby. Just be yourself and… "

BOOOOOOOOOOOOOOOOOOOOOO…

As her campaign manager continued to fret, that blustering boob, Bailey—with both thumbs in plaster casts—stole a sidelong glance at her, while climbing a short flight of stairs to the debate stage, then sheepishly turned his blackened eyes away.

BOOOOOOOOOOOOOOOOOOOOOOOOOOOOOO…

"Remember, Hilde," Maude hissed in her ear, "Bailey is your first target, but he's only a rabbit-puncher, at best. If you come out swinging like we practiced, he's sure to cry 'Uncle' and throw in the towel. Save your best shots for later rounds against… "

We want Henry! We want Henry! We want Henry!

My God, Jonathan Henry came toward her, wearing the pants of her sky-blue pantsuit! At peddle-pusher length on him, they were somewhat flattering to his tall figure, though obviously stretched out of shape and baggy in the rear, damnit! Printed on his white baseball cap: *Cowgirls Like to Get Bucked!* She turned away, but halfway up the stairs felt him pressing against her buttocks, where that stupid Oklahoma State college slogan on her orange leisure suit said *RIDE 'EM!* "Bohica!," he said from over her shoulder. "Bend over, Little Beaver, here it comes again."

We want Etta! We want Etta! We want Etta!

We want Henry! We want Henry! We want Henry!

Unnerved, Hilde walked onto the stage and... involuntarily blinked her lensless brown eye at the sight of—not Judy Woodruff at the media table beside Rachel Maddow—but that little strawberry blonde snoop who worked for the local newspaper. And on her other side... Shit! Another absurdly long-haired blonde woman, whom she vaguely recognized as a Fox News propagandist for the vast right-wing conspiracy. Jonathan Henry crossed the stage to the long, lean bitch like a puppy, knelt on one knee, and licked her extended paw!

Bow-wow-wow-wow!

Me-ow -wow-wow!

Resisting an urge to similarly suck-up to Rachel, Hilde turned toward the audience, with a surprised but undelighted frown at Maude on the front row, who idiotically grinned and made a punching motion with a clinched fist.

Sic 'em! Sic 'em! Sic em!

Let the big dog eat! Let the big dog eat! Let the big dog eat!

In a stunned daze, she barely grasped the so-called rules announced by the so-called debate moderator: Something about Jonathan Henry to be the designated "home team" on the gym scoreboard, she the "visitor," and any points for or against Bailey to be counted on someone's fingers.

BUZZ!

Startled out of her stupor, Hilde regained her presence of mind. "I am no la-dy," she announced, having expected she would be introduced by the term. "I am wo-man! And as a wo-man, I demand that Mayor Bailey be re-moved from this stage and dis-qualified from seeking high office for commission of a sexual ass-ault on your be-loved Aunt Maude!"

Boo, boo, boo...

"Not a chance," said Jonathan Henry, now standing behind a podium to her right. "For cryin' out loud, just look at that face," he said, sweeping an arm in Maude's direction. "Not even our hard-up Mayor, whose mother, by the way, probably put those mittens on him for obvious reasons, could get it up for Maude Rouser."

Rah, rah, rah...

BUZZ!

"One point for Mr. Henry, none for Ms. Bottomly, none for Mayor Bailey," the obviously biased moderator announced. "Aunt Maude got even with the Mayor, and they settled their differences at the police station after a public rasslin' match."

Rah, rah, rah...

Hilde mentally thumbed through a memorized list of talking points. "I am wo-man!" she said. "And as a wom-an, I de-mand that Mayor Bailey be im-peached right this very minute, for shacking up with an illegal Mexican maiden. A man who abuses his position of authority over a lowly fe-male is unfit for high office."

Ha, ha, ha, ha, ha, ha, ha, ha, ha, ha... ... .

"No way, Jose," Jonathan Henry said, again coming to the defense of his unlikely BFF, Bailey. "Unfortunately, our current Mayor is only a masturbator, that's what's wrong with this town. So he has to go, but by vote of citizens in tomorrow's three-way election. On the other hand, women are incredibly crazy over me, they tell me all the time: Jonathan, you drive me crazy. I could mention names, but don't want to embarrass anyone else on stage."

Ha, ha, ha, ha, ha, ha...

BUZZ!

"Minus one point against Mr. Henry, for bringin' up

Mayor Bailey's mama, and mittens. Minus one point against Ms. Bottomly, for bringin' up a possibly illegal, and no doubt desperately lonely Mexican maiden. Two fingers in favor of the Mayor for doin' his best to break a youthful habit."

Ha, ha, ha, ha, ha, ha…

Hilde considered, but decided against making a personal attack against the pesky little moderator, who had admitted to being engaged to marry a prison convict. Determined to stay on message, she again mentally took stock of her campaign talking points and… "I am wo-man! " she said, to no applause from the audience, nor buzz for award of a debate point. Only prolonged silence followed her proclamation, even though she would be the first woman elected Mayor of this wretched town.

"Ms. Moon Bottomly," the Fox News sniper said—Hilde braced herself for a biased attack—"you and your husband are co-founders of the Homes Sweet Homes Foundation in Washington, I am told, which is affiliated with Ms. Maude Rouser's local association of the same name that set up a 'sanctuary' neighborhood in this town, where illegal Mexican rapists are reportedly allowed to work on a vegetable farm, and get paid in American dollars, rather than receive forty lashes a day. What do you have to say in defense of your treason?"

Boooooooooo…

"I have no connection to my husband's business, and have not laid eyes nor any other body part on him in months," Hilde firmly answered. "As for… Did you say 'Maude Rouser'? Oh yes, she was a high school classmate, and more recently a rape victim, whom I hardly know."

BUZZ! BUZZ! BUZZ!

"Three points against Ms. Moon Bottomly!

Rah, rah, rah, rah, rah, rah, rah, rah, rah, rah, rah, rah, rah…

THIRTY SEVEN

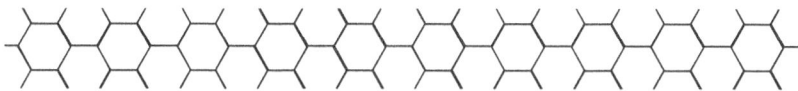

Henryetta felt a hard tap on her shoulder, swiveled her head and saw it was Ms. By-God Mercer, who had come up on the debate stage behind her. "Hey, cupcake," she said in a semi-lowered voice, "did that big swinging dick, Henry, get to you, or are you in the tank for that asshole, Bailey?" She knew of course what the League of Women Voters organizer was talking about, but... Dang it, semi-helping things along in Ms. Bottomly's direction was like trying to steer a fully loaded dump truck down a slick muddy road. "I myself would not knock a lung out of a little runt like you," the goonish gal said, "but my daughter, Lateesha, might just come down here and raise a pop-knot on your head, big enough for a calf to suck on. It aint nothin' for my little girl to whup a man's ass." Henryetta got the message, same as Mr. Harold had got it the other day, but...

"Where do you stand on same-sex marriage, Mr. Henry?" Ms. Maddow asked. "My guess is that you would oppose erection of a statue in this town in honor of... "

BUZZ!

"Three points against Ms. Maddow," Henryetta declared. "The Supreme Court has already decided that issue, and besides: It's only rumor that the statue of a local hero will be wearing a dress, or even that it's really gay."

Rah, rah, rah...

"But gettin' back to gender matters, Ms. Bottomly," said Henryetta, before Ms. Rachel could say more about the Gaylord issue, "where do you stand on the question of a transgender gal's constitutional right to urinate any place she wants to?"

Ms. Bottomly eyed her like she thought the soft ball throwed at her had a gob of spit on it. "For your information, I do <u>not</u> <u>stand</u> for urination anywhere," she said, cold as a side of beef hanging in a meat locker. "I am wo-man! Suggestions to the contrary are baseless rumors put out by biased so-called news reporters, such as you."

Rah, rah, rah...

BUZZ!

"Three points for Ms. Bottomly!

Boo, boo, boo...

"What the hell is this, a fair debate or an all-girl pissing contest?" Mr. Henry complained, appealing to the audience with wide-spread arms.

Rah, rah, rah...

"You know, I own the bonds put out to build this gym. If people don't start being nice to me, I'll foreclose in a New York minute. Believe me, I'm a great forecloser, I've made a fortune kicking deadbeat tenants off my properties. By tomorrow, I'll make an amazing deal for, say, a whore house in this building. I've made a fortune... "

Boo, boo, boo...

Rah, rah, rah...

Boo, boo, boo...

"Oh, for cryin' out loud, gimme a break," said Ms. Bottomly, who seemed to have forgot her Okie accent. "He's nothing but a freakin' Elvis impersonator, his riff is from a childhood movie," she said, before swiveling her broadish hips and starting into a deep-throated Elvis impersonator show of her own: "When I walk through that door/ baby be polite/ You're gonna make me sore/ if you don't treat me right... "

Rah, rah, rah...

"You can't sing, but you do look like Elvis," Mr. Henry said, "in his later, grossly *zaftig* years. I'll give you that."

Boo, boo, boo...

"Make me feel at home/ if you really care/ Scratch my back and run your pretty/ fingers through my hair... "

Rah, rah, rah...

"You wish, but no chance. And by the way, Zafty, if I were you I wouldn't be crooning that particular tune. It's from *Jailhouse Rock*."

Booooooo...

"...treat me nice."

Rah, rah, rah...
Boo, boo, boo...
Rah, rah, rah...
BUZZ!

"Two points for Ms. Bottomly, on account of good acting like she was someone else."

The Jonathan puckered his lips and gave her the stink eye. "By the way," he said, "I also own the building where a certain little hair house is located. Not that I would ever be caught dead in that estrogen pit. My man, Tonto, styles my hair, and he is amazing, absolutely incredible, as anyone can see. I'm not just another pretty face, I'm the only pretty face on this stage."

Rah, rah, rah...
BUZZ!

"Two more points for Ms. Bottomly! And a half-point for Aunt Maude!"

Boo, boo, boo...

"What about pot holes?!" someone in the audience shouted. And only then did Henryetta notice that Mayor Bailey was still on the stage, looking like a cornered black-eyed raccoon and semi-twiddling his plastered thumbs.

THIRTY
EIGHT

Jonathan looked at his watch. He was of a mind similar to that of the President of Turkey, or maybe it was the Mayor of Chicago who likened democracy to a train: When you got to where you wanted to go, you got off. Though actual voting would not happen 'til tomorrow, he had already put enough sludge in the system to feel the so-called democratic process slowing to almost a halt in his favor. Only out of respect for Miss Ann had he put up with almost an hour of meaningless bullroar. And the so-called debate had not even gotten to the only matter of any importance to him: Re-naming the town in his, technically also in his great grandfather's honor. At the outset of tonight's wing-ding, on bended knee, he had invited Miss Ann to come up to his penthouse afterward. Ladylike, she'd reacted with only a cooly stand-offish nasal purr, but now... Feeling itchier, he again checked the time, looked up and winked at the long, lean cougar. Hot damn, he loved the haughtiness of those blank, catlike, pale blue eyes. Interrupting the whiny drone of his female opponent about something, he addressed the Fox News cougar:

"When you're next in town, Miss Ann, you won't have to worry about that sanctuary neighborhood put up by these two sissies," he said, with a glance at his debate opponents. "As

Mayor, I will clear Kellogg's Korner of every living thing in sight. And by the way, back in New York you'll be able to sleep at night without fear of being attacked by any Mexican rapers, soon as I put up a brick shit-house of a wall across the eastbound Interstate. I've already made a deal with FEMA to store fifty thousand mobile houses on my land north of town. Believe me, it won't be a country club. There will be no 'anchor babies' made on my watch. I'll work the SWOPs night and day so hard, they'll pay double the costs of charter buses to take 'em back across the border. You'll be absolutely amazed."

No anchor babies! No anchor babies! No anchor babies!

"Be still, my heart," Miss Ann drawled through her nose. "I look forward to seeing your 'tent city' sketches later on, Mr. Henry, in private."

Rah, rah, rah…

BUZZ!

"Minus two points for Mr. Henry, for interrupting. Go on with what you were sayin', Ms. Bottomly."

"As I was about to say, Mr. Henry, who happens to be a high school classmate of mine—nicknamed 'Stinky,' by the way—was voted 'Most Likely to End Up Broke'. No doubt he would now be penniless if he had not preyed on the misfortunes of others, including the citizens of this town, who were most recently swindled by him and Mayor Bailey in an under-the-table deal to unload the broken-down Bunkhouse Motel—which he acquired by inheritance—onto the backs of local taxpayers, mainly hard working women."

Boo, boo, boo…

BUZZ!

"Another good point for Ms. Bottomly. Your turn, Ms. Rachel."

Rah, rah, rah… Fight, fight, fight…

"Thank you, Miss Henryetta," the panel's obviously 'transgendered' person said, with a viciously sweet, obviously fake smile. "Mr. Henry, I'm told you were born an already rich Little Lord Fauntleroy, flunked out of reform school, and that your only 'qualifications' for public office are that you are an outsider, not an experienced politician but only a businessman. And yet, your only known idea for local economic development, endorsed by Mayor Bailey, is to 'build' a nuclear waste dump in the middle of town, which can only have disastrous effects, not only on people but for the local economy. What's the deal, schlemiel?"

Boo, boo, boo…

Jonathan held out his arms and upturned palms to the so-called moderator of the so-called debate. "Who is this sissy-boy?" he asked, before turning on the he/she questioner and… Reminded that this was only politics, he decided to make nice. "If you were rich like me, and knew business from biscuits, you wouldn't ask such a stupid question," he said to "Ms./Mr. Rachel," with a matching fake smile. "My nuclear waste facility will bring hundreds of truckers into town, every day, three hundred sixty-five days a year. Truck drivers need to eat, they get hungry for fast food when they're on the road. And they get bored steering those loaded eighteen-wheelers, so they need porn to help kill time while passing slow-moving non-commercial vehicles, which by the way, don't pay squat for highway construction and maintenance. Believe me, *XXX* porn parlors lining both sides of Main Street will pay a helluva lot more sales taxes, and rent, than hardware stores, beauty shops and day-care joints. It will be so amazing, so incredible for the town, it will make your already dizzy head spin."

Rah, rah, rah, rah, rah, rah, rah, rah, rah, rah, rah, rah…
BUZZ!

"Minus five points for Mr. Henry. Minus a finger for Mayor Bailey."

Boo, boo, boo, boo, boo, boo, boo, boo, boo, booooooo…

Jonathan looked toward Miss Ann, who seemed to be packing papers into a brief case. Was she getting ready to leave? He had not wanted to go nuclear, which could be risky, but Little Beaver had obviously leaked his high school record and… Miss Ann was now standing, damnit. Earlier that day, he had come upon an old high school yearbook, *The Squab/1965*, still sealed in plastic paper. He'd unwrapped the thin volume and, for use in case of emergency, had Xeroxed a single page… Miss Ann had started toward an exit.

"Little Beaver was never a real Indian princess," he bellowed. "And she is not an experienced politician. I have printed proof," he said, taking the Xerox from a jacket pocket, "that she was not elected President of the Student Council, like she claims!"

Boo, boo, boo…

"The football jocks stuffed the ballot box!" Little Beaver shouted. "I deserved to be elected and…"

Boo, boo, boo…

"She came to me for 'backing', but I got behind her <u>good</u> looking opponent, and…"

"…my father told me I was an Indian princess and called me Little Beaver!"

Boo, boo, boo…
BUZZ!

"And that's not all," Jonathan shouted, at the sight of Miss Ann returning to the media table. "My opponent only got into a junior college for dumb girls, not Wellesley, and…"

"Pine Manor was located in the town of Wellesley back then, and not all the girls… "

"…in high school, she was nicknamed 'Fatso,' in Yiddish, and voted 'Most Likely to End Up In Jail'!"

Boo, boo, boo…

BUZZ! BUZZ! BUZZ!

Rah, rah, rah…

BUZZ! BUZZ! BUZZ!

Rah, rah, rah, rah, rah, rah, rah, rah, rah, rah…

From the enraptured expression in Miss Ann's eyes, not to mention her enthusiastic cheering, Jonathan had no doubt he had sealed the deal. He was amazing, he was so absolutely incredible it made his head spin.

THIRTY NINE

Henryetta looked up at the gym scoreboard. Ms. Bottomly, the "visitor," was way ahead, not much time was left on the game clock, and whether to change or not change the high school mascot and town name—which was what she her own self cared most about—had not yet been debated. "Ms. Bottomly," she said, "awhile back, on this here stage, you declared that a Republican War on Women has been goin' on in town since at least 1989, when a bunch of boys got together and changed our mascot to... " A fella from PBS TV came onstage and handed Henryetta a piece of paper. It was headed *AP NEWS BULLETIN* and said... Oh no... She looked over at poor Ms. Bottomly, already shrouded in a black lace headscarf. Should she break the bad news to the wo-man candidate now or wait "til... Miss Ann reached over and grabbed the bulletin. A wicked smile crossed her face as she scanned what was wrote on the paper.

"Ms. <u>Moon</u> Bottomly," she said, "I'm sure you will be relieved to hear that your wayward spouse, Mr. William "Buddy" Moon—on the lam from federal authorities for weeks—has been found... "

Rah, rah, rah...

"... washed up on a beach in Cabo San Lucas, Mexico... "

Oooooooo...

"... alive and well."

Rah, rah, rah...

In reaction to the news reported by Miss Ann, a tear ran down Ms. Bottomly's cheek, dropped onto a black *OSU Cowboys* patch stuck to a front pocket of her orange outfit, and... Land sakes alive, one of her eyes had turned brown!

"According to the *AP*," Miss Ann continued, with her own two blue eyes bright as headlights on high beam, "your 'Buddy' was caught *en flagrante,* trying to 'keep it up' with multiple Khardashians."

Ooooooooooooooooooooooooooooooooooo...

Obviously in shock, Ms. Moon Bottomly adjusted her scarf and... "Sometimes it's hard to be a wo-man," she semi-groaned, "giving all your love to just one man. You'll have bad times, and he'll have good times, doin' things you don't understand. But if you love him... "

"Oh, and this news too," said Miss Ann, looking at the *AP* Bulletin. "Reportedly, Mr. Moon is cooperating with a congressional committee investigating bad deeds committed by him and <u>other</u> officials of the Homes Sweet Homes Foundation. Any comment, Ms. <u>Moon</u> Bottomly?"

"I aint no little ol' Tammy Wyn-ette," the wronged wife answered, throwing off her black head cover. "I am wom-an, an independent Dicksy Chick and Fighting Hen, who will not stand up or fall down beside any man!"

Rah, rah, rah, rah, rah, rah, rah, rah, rah, rah, rah, rah...
We want Etta! We want Etta! We want Etta!
BUZZ!

"Ten points for... "

"Fighting Dicksy Chicken, my ass!" Jonathan Henry bellowed,

before commencing a longwinded speech about town history and a local man named Frank Shurden, who—according to Mr. Henry—once upon a time was a State Senator from Okmulgee County, and had got national news media attention for putting up legislation to re-legalize cockfighting. "Shurden, who is also a manly rancher, by the way, had his head pointed in the right direction," Mr. Henry said, "but he was a Democrat—of the Blue Dog breed, but still, a Democrat, and a politician—who tried to satisfy all those sissies at the State Capitol with a wishy-washy compromise requiring the cocks to wear miniature boxing gloves."

Boo, boo, boo, boo, boo, boo, boo, boo...

"Soon as I take office as Mayor, the gloves come off, the cocks come out, and we fight, fight, fight for dear old HHS!"

Rah, rah, rah, rah, rah, rah, rah, rah, rah, rah, rah, rah, rah, rah...

Gloves off! Cocks out! Gloves off! Cocks out!

Fighting Cocks! Fighting Cocks! Fighting Cocks!

Fight! Fight! Fight!

BUZZ! BUZZ! BUZZ!

And when those Fighting Cocks take the field/ we'll fight, fight, fight... .

Hens!

Cocks!

Hens!

Cocks!

Fight! Fight! Fight!...

That mascot idea of Mr. Henry's might just about settle the whole dern election, Henryetta reckoned. It looked to her like Ms. Bottomly and Etta were likely to be losers, but at least the town wouldn't be called Henryetta no more. And that was a mercy.

FORTY

As Buford's two opponents and town voters kept on hollering about the town name and mascot, he continued to remain calm. Waiting for just the right moment to jerk his rabbit—that was not actually the mascot he'd settled on—out of a hat, just figuratively speaking—he had stifled a slight, but detectable surge of testosterone when that female "visitor," Ms. Bottomly, accused him of making improper advances at Aunt Maude. He'd also resisted an urge to punch her in the nose when she claimed he was "shacked up" with a Mexican woman, partly because he took it as a compliment, partly because the semi-youngish Maria had smiled at him from her front row seat without seeming to have felt insulted, partly because his broken thumbs still hurt. And though he had found that real estate taxes on her Division Street house had for years been paid, probably improperly, by Aunt Maude's Home Sweet Homes Association, he'd held his water when Ms. Bottomly got tangled up in her husband's scandal. Now, finally, with the important election issues of town mascot and name on the table, his powder was dry and Buford was ready to fight, fight, fight for his political life.

"Are you freaking crazy?" the Bottomly woman now shrieked at Mr. Henry. "Your great grandpa Hugh was a Confederate soldier, for cryin' out loud, a buffalo hunter to boot, and you yourself admitted he was a drunkard!"

Boo, boo, boo...

BUZZ!

"Two points against Mr. Henry and his great grandpa."

Boo, boo, boo...

"All I 'admitted' was that the conniving postmaster, Etta Beard, was likely the little minx who got him drunk, so she and her husband could cheat Great Grandpa Hugh out of my land. And by the way, when it comes to family, a liquored up Johnny Reb is a heckuva lot more respectable than a jailbird husband, in cahoots with a certain candidate on this stage that I am too much of a gentleman to mention by name."

Rah, rah, rah...

BUZZ!

"Two points for Ms. Bottomly, one for the Post Office Madam, Ms. Beard, and... Is that a finger raised there next to your thumb, Mayor Bailey? Have you finally thought of somethin' to say?"

BOOOOOOOOOOOOOOOOOOOOOOOOOO...

"Thank you, fellow citizens, one and all," Buford said, after being reassured to see that the semi-youngish Mexican Maria seemed to be shouting *Ole! Ole! Ole!* "As someone once said: Campaigning for high public office, making up reasons why someone should vote for you, is like spouting poetry, while actually holding public office is doing things that don't have rhyme or reason. In other words, while my two opponents have been just talking about old and new town names and mascots, as your Mayor, I have been at work with a certain Mr. Doolittle in Dallas. And I am proud and pleased to announce that tomorrow morning, on your way to the polls, you will pass by two statues on Main Street. One of local hero... "

"What about the pot holes, Booster?!" someone shouted.

"As a wo-man, I find unkempt holes sexist, and inexcusably

offensive."

Rah, rah rah.

"As Mayor, I'll make every pot hole in town amazing, absolutely incredible."

Rah, rah, rah.

"One of the statues honors hometown hero, Troy Aikman," Buford continued. "The other pays tribute to hometown hero, Gaylord Goodhart. Both went onto fame and fortune as Dallas Cowboys. In addition..."

Rah, rah, rah...

BUZZ!

"No points against you yet, Mr. Mayor, but we're runnin' out of time, so I'll have to dock you if you don't change the subject and get more short-winded."

"In addition to Aikman and Goodhart," Buford re-continued, "our town has another homegrown hero who we sometimes forget: Mr. Jim Shoulders, the greatest rodeo champion in history."

Rah, rah, rah, rah, rah, rah, rah, rah...

Ride 'em, cowboy!

Rah, rah, rah, rah, rah...

Yippee-ki-yi-yo!

Rah, rah, rah, rah, rah, rah, rah, rah...

Buford's confidence surged. "Now, I have not yet lined up a statue of actually Mr. Shoulders," he yelled. "But the World War I Doughboy in front of the library could be moved into the street, at no taxpayer expense to speak of. We could paint Mr. Jim's name on it, and at three straight intersections—at 4th, 5th and 6th Streets—have three famous cowboys, who... "

"Cow<u>boy</u> mascot?!" Ms. Bottomly screeched. "Absolutely not! Damnit, Adam got to name all the animals in the Garden of Eden—from Wildcats to Tigers to the Fighting Skeeters—and then took it upon himself to name wo-man Eve. It's my turn, and damnit, I want everyone in town to be known as Fighting Hens!"

Booooooooooooo...

"Okay, let's make a deal and wrap this up," Mr. Henry said, as the log-haired blonde quizzer, Miss Coulter, again got up from the newspersons' table. "You and your kind can be Hens," he said to Ms. Bottomly. "I and the town's other males will be Fighting Cocks. Bailey can be whatever... "

Rah, rah, rah...

"Statues!" Buford shouted, with both plastered thumbs raised over his head. The crowd got quiet. "For a mascot, I hereby officially nominate **Fighting Statues**! And for the name of the town... "

Henryetta Fighting Statues!

Rah, rah, rah, rah, rah, rah, rah...

Henryetta Fighting Statues!

Bailey! Bailey! Bailey!

Henryetta Fighting Statues!

Rah, rah, rah...

Bailey! Bailey! Bailey!

The semi-younger Mexican Maria rushed onstage to stand by him. To Buford's further surprise, and alarm, he felt himself being lifted into the air. As he had never before even dared to dream, a rabble of townsfolk carried him on their shoulders out of the gym—where he had never so much as bounced a ball—shouting: *BAI-LEY! BAI-LEY! BAI-LEY!*

Inspired by the outpouring of both male and female voter support, Buford's mind settled on retaining the name Henryetta for the town, then turned to seeking higher office immediately after his re-election to a new four-year term as Mayor.

THAT WHICH WE CALL A ROSE
BY ANY OTHER NAME WOULD
SMELL AS SWEET.

William Shakespeare/ Romeo & Juliet

FORTY ONE

After the polls closed on Election Day, Henryetta sat at her same old *Weekly Herald* desk, waiting for the Election Board boss lady to call. Based on what everybody in town seemed to think was his "strong debate performance," Mayor Bailey was likely to win the vote count, she reckoned. So nothing was likely to change, not the town name, and not even the local mascot. Gaylord's plaster likeness had showed up—in pants, Praise the Lord—but already one of his legs had got knocked off, by a Russ-the-Plumber truck hurrying to an overflow emergency. And other unsightly overflow from birds was already piling up on both stark white "Fighting Statues." But the election had served a purpose, she supposed; at least that was what today's *New York Times* said would likely be the case in its regular **READ IT NOW: NEWS FROM THE WAR FRONT** column, that must have been wrote down early last night before the big debate. Though Henryetta had already looked at the piece, she decided she ought to read it again now:

HENRYETTA | OKLAHOMA - *This hinterland hamlet is a lot like London in 1944, only worse in many respects. Here in America's heartland, the Republican Party blitzkrieg launched in 1964 under the ruthless command of Air Force General Barry Goldwater has* *already resulted in a half century of Nazi occupation. Until recently, the brave resistance movement led by former Oklahoma Democratic Senator Fred Harris, carrying a "No More Bullshit" banner, was all but forgotten. African-Americans, women, homosexuals, transgender urinators and other minorities have been virtually consigned to P.O.W. camps. Yes, Democrats rose up against their oppressors four years ago, out of an underground movement that produced a Vice-Presidential candidate named Virgil Carter, but only to be crushed under the thumb of a Republican apparatchik, the infamous town Mayor, Buford Bailey. Hope of liberating voters and bringing them back into the fold of the Democratic Party for next year's Presidential election appeared lost, until a brave and charismatic female person of the people entered this year's local Mayoral battle and took a courageous stand in the War on Women.*

Henryetta again peeked at the column's bottom to re-confirm that Benjamin Bortz had not been credited as a contributor to the piece, and again saw there was no newly listed e-mail address where she could reach him. Dang it! Earlier in the day, she had got around to looking up who in tarnation the Nacirema people were and what they were up to. Now she was both relieved and aggravated at Benjamin Bortz for not telling, or not knowing, that *Nacirema* was *American*, spelled backward. The so-called "Prophet Horace" was a famous sociologist, who had come up with the term *Nacirema* to create "objective detachment" in the way Americans looked at theirselves and their own ways, which to other so-called primitive people must seem odd as socks on a rooster.

The "Nacirema Magical Beliefs and Body Rituals" that plain ol' Horace Miner described, and Benjamin passed on, were mainly about Americans' bathroom habits inside household "shrines," the focal points of which were "fonts"—meaning plain ol' lavatories—and above them, built-in boxes or chests for keeping "charms and magical powder for preservation of worshipers." They, the built-in boxes, were plain ol' medicine chests, or maybe what Benjamin would call *Beau Brummell* portmanteaus. That was the relieving, but also aggravating part of her research. She'd not found anything about a "Church of the Holy Cow," and was still worried to distraction about what Billy Ray's big-breasted mamas and his daddy, The Mister, might have done to conform Gaylie for a same-sex wedding.

Henryetta looked up at a wall calendar. Only ten days from now, she was supposed to show up at halftime of a football game in Dallas for a Ring of Honor ceremony—wearing in a tuxedo—to be the "Best Man." Unless a miracle happened…

To take her mind off the likely awful truth, she went back to the *New York Times* piece. Again, she read that prior to last night's debate Ms. Bottomly had inspired both local women and Mexican volunteer freedom fighters to join her crusade to change the town name to Etta and restore its feminist mascot to Fighting Hens; how Mayor Bailey, fearing he would be hanged by his neck for committing war crimes against women, had gone into hiding and possibly fled the county; and how a jackbooted band of angry, white male storm troopers on the payroll of a capitalist pig, Jonathan Armstrong Henry, had led a rebellion within the Republican Party and launched a counter-attack against Ms. Bottomly's "Pink Revolution." Ordinarily, in reaction to *New York Times* reporting and commentary, Henryetta felt ashamed to be too ignorant to have previously understood things she her own self had seen with her own eyes or heard with her own ears. But in this particular case, she began to think …

Later tonight, forces on both sides are massed here on the windswept Plains of Oklahoma for a veritable Battle of Armageddon, sponsored by the League of Women Voters and PBS. Outcome of this odd-year clash of good versus evil could well foretell or forebode the outcome of next year's Presidential election.

Good night, America, and good luck.

Some doubtful that she her own self would ever become a reporter for a big city newspaper, Henryetta nevertheless folded up **NEWS FROM THE WAR FRONT** for her learning scrapbook, and... *Buzz... Buzz... Buzz...* Land sakes alive! It was Benjamin Bortz calling!

"Sorry to have been out of touch, Henryetta," he said, breezy as a short skirt in March. "Gaylord and I have been on lock-down, strictly *incommunicado*."

Lock-down? Henryetta had never heard of "Communicado," but reckoned it must be a place in Mexico, maybe where a pink double-domed "Mother" Church of the Holy Cow was located. In answer to her asking about Gaylord, "I'm fine and dandy," Benjamin answered, "never better, in fact. And so is Gaylie." In answer to her follow-up question about conformation, "I held Gaylie's hand through the entire wonderful process, and came to see the light myself. Neither of us is any more a *Hugo Boss* man than a *Nike* man. The great Gaylord Goodhart and the great I are natural-reborn *Nacirema* men, both conformed members of the Church of the Holy Cow."

Oh no, Henryetta felt responsible in some way for involving Benjamin in Gaylord's peculiarities.

"Together, we're launching a whole new line," he said, "under the brand, get this: *THE MISTER'S PORTMANTEAU, Natural Nacirema Product for the New Metrosexual Male.* Catchy, huh?"

Henryetta reckoned the news could have been worse, but still wondered... "And hey, Henryetta, guess what else? I'm getting fitted tomorrow in a unisex *Chris Dior* original, for the big wedding. Billy Ray has asked me to be his, you know, 'BFF of Honor'. So I will see you soon, in the Ring of Honor."

That was about all the good news Henryetta could stand, but before she could end the call... "And by the way, Henryetta, based on all your Gaylord stories going back to the beginning of your relationship, my *Times* piece has turned into a book—titled *Gaylord and Me, From My Unique Personal Perspective*—and my agent thinks it has the right stuff for a Pulitzer. But don't worry, you're not mentioned by name. See you in Dallas." Click.

Henryetta sighed, enjoyed a personal pity party for a second or two, then went to opening mail that had piled up. About halfway down the stack of mostly bills, she came across a largish envelope, addressed to her personally. She opened it and...

Buzz... Buzz... Buzz...

The call was coming from the Election Board, likely to report the outcome of the Mayoral contest, but she was in no hurry to take it. In her hand, she already had what she wanted: A fancy Okmulgee County Court certificate that officially changed her name to a feminine *HENRIETTA*, with an i right there where a y used to be.

Buzz... buzz... Buzz...

If there ever was any curse put on her, by her mother, Wynona Sue— on purpose or not—or by her Cajun grandma, or by an Okmulgee County clerk who mis-typed her birth certificate, now it was gone up in smoke. And yet, "Henrietta" felt like nothing much had changed, and likely never would.

Buzz... Buzz... Buzz...

THE END

www.ingramcontent.com/pod-product-compliance
Lightning Source LLC
Chambersburg PA
CBHW031309170626
46807CB00001B/344